Watch *and* LEARN

K.C. WELLS

Watch and Learn
Cover Art by Meredith Russell
Photo by Wander Aguiar

This story was originally published as part of the Come Play anthology.
It has since been expanded from 14,000 to 28,000 words.

Cover content is being used for illustrative purposes only and any person depicted on the cover is a model.

"Fucking is a dying art."

"Say, if you really wanna clean my bar top with your tongue, I can go with that."

That brought Chris Levinson down to earth with not just a bump, but a resounding *smack*. He gave the bartender a '*What the fuck?*' glance, which apparently cut no ice with Bill, as his badge proclaimed.

Bill shrugged. "Well, you've been drooling over that guy for the last half hour. I figured you might as well do something useful with your tongue." His eyes sparkled. "Or… you could go over there and just *talk* to the guy. I hear that approach works pretty well too."

"You obviously took up bar-tending because you failed as a comedian, right?" Chris gestured to his empty glass. "I'll have another. And get him another of whatever *he's* having," he added, pointing to the young man at the far end of the bar.

Bill quirked his eyebrows. "Finally gonna make a move, huh?"

Chris could've told Bill he had it all wrong, but decided in the end he wasn't worth the breath. He waited until Bill placed the full glass in front of the young man before raising his own.

The guy stared at him, a slight frown creasing his forehead.

Chris took that as his cue to move. He slid off his bar stool, picked up his glass, and walked unhurriedly to the far end of the bar, where the young man was watching his approach cautiously. When Chris reached him, he perched on the empty stool beside him and put down his glass. He said nothing.

The younger man looked him up and down, then tilted his head to one side. "Do I know you?" Pale brown eyes focused on him, that frown still evident.

"No, but after seeing you in that same damn spot every Friday night for the past month, with that same expression, I couldn't take anymore. I had to find a way to talk to you." Chris didn't believe in beating around the bush. He was too long in the tooth to be indulging in small talk.

Mr. Brown Eyes lifted his eyebrows. "What expression would that be?"

Chris went for the jugular. "The one that says you're not happy."

He gave a blink, then recovered, smirking. "And who are you, the Happiness Fairy? You gonna sprinkle some fairy dust and take *all* my troubles away?"

"I'm the guy who's gonna sit next to you and listen while you tell me what's on your mind. Because *something* sure is." Chris's gaze flickered around the rest of the bar, where all types of men indulged in drinking, chatting, flirting or in some cases, making out. Of course, no one batted an eyelid at the latter.

This was New York City, for God's sake.

"Maybe I'm just having a bad day," the young man suggested.

Chris shook his head. "It's not just today, though. I told you, I've watched you for the past four Fridays. You sit there, you drink. Occasionally you dance. Sometimes, you flirt. And at the end of the night, you leave with a guy."

The man stiffened. "Something wrong with that?"

"Fuck no. At least half the guys in this bar are here to hook up with someone. Me included. Not a thing wrong with that. What gets to me about *you* is that you're clearly looking for something and you can't seem to find it." He smiled. "Now, we could go on like this all night, back and forth, *or* you could tell me your name, I'll tell you mine, we'll have a drink, and we'll talk."

Chris couldn't miss the amusement dancing briefly in those pretty eyes. "Talk. You just wanna… talk."

"It's a start," Chris said with a shrug. He took a drink of his beer.

After a moment, the guy picked up his glass and took a drink. When he put it down, he met Chris's gaze. "What the hell. My name's Zac. Zac Tanner."

Chris smiled. "That's better. I'm Chris Levinson. I'm forty-two. I'm getting it out there now, because I know you're gonna ask at some point."

Zac arched his eyebrows. "You sure don't *look* forty-two. I'd have said thirty-five, tops."

"I'm gonna take that as a compliment. Okay, back to my bio. No boyfriends. No partners. Not interested in that. Been there, done that. Plenty of guys out there, just looking for a good time."

Zac expelled a long breath, and to Chris's mind, it was a release of tension. He leaned against the bar, his spine less rigid. "I'm twenty-two. No boyfriend. No partner." He paused to take a drink. "And seriously considering taking a vow of celibacy."

Okay, Chris hadn't expected *that*. Zac's age had surprised him too. Chris had thought him closer to his mid-twenties. He was a good-looking guy, with a tangle of dirty blond curls on top, short at the sides. Definitely no stranger to a gym, judging by those shoulders.

Chris *loved* it when a guy worked out.

He chuckled. "At twenty-two? Wow." Then he

regretted his reaction. Judging by Zac's expression, he was deadly serious. Chris cleared his throat. "Okay. That's not something I usually hear from a guy your age, so I'm guessing there's a story behind it. Well, why don't you tell me?"

Zac regarded him steadily. "What it all boils down to is… I've come to the conclusion that fucking is a dying art." He took another drink.

This time Chris met his words with a slow nod. "Okay. Not saying I agree with you on this one, but I'd sure be interested to know what brought you to this particular conclusion." He downed a mouthful of beer before continuing. "Can I ask questions?"

"Sure."

"How many guys have you been involved with?"

Zac snorted. "Is that a euphemism for fucked? Hooked-up with? Screwed? Because involvement implies a degree of connection, and I've never had that."

Something inside Chris clenched at those matter-of-fact words. Before he could get another word out, however, Zac plunged ahead.

"Sorry if that sounds harsh, but hey, I kinda got the impression we weren't dicking around here. I thought you wanted to hear the truth, rather than some prettied-up version of it."

"You got that right." Chris liked Zac already.

Zac gave a satisfied nod. "That's why I'm still here. It's refreshing not to have to wade through a load of bullshit."

"And forgive me. I assumed you were gay. For all I know, you're bi."

Zac shook his head. "Nah. You had me nailed right. I knew I was gay from the age of fourteen. But you asked a question, so let me answer it as fully as I can. I got laid for the first time when I was sixteen. He was a jock on the school football team, and I was his little experiment, only not a very successful one. He didn't have a clue what he was doing."

"None of us do at that age," Chris remarked. "The hormones take over and it's mostly a case of 'yay, there's a hole.' I take it the experience wasn't good?"

Zac winced. "Can we say, 'where's the lube'?"

Aw fuck. Chris's ass contracted just thinking about it. "Ouch."

"Let's just say it was a while before I even thought about doing it again. And definitely not with him."

"So… next guy."

Zac nodded. "And I topped. It was… kinda meh. Mind you, we only had like ten minutes to do it. Can't even remember why now. And then I sorta got into a pattern of crappy dates and even crappier sex."

"What was bad about them, specifically?"

Zac huffed out a breath. "I guess I just haven't been lucky with my choice of guys. I mean, it didn't take me long to work out I was a bottom, and I really thought things would get better. But… no one ever seemed to take the time to… arouse me, y'know? It was like foreplay was a dirty word. And when there *was* some, it was never enough. And don't get me started on their stamina. Three minutes, tops, and they were done. Meanwhile, I'm lying there with my knees at my ears, waiting for the fireworks to begin. Only, they didn't. Hell, I didn't even get my fuse lit." His face fell. "Is it so much to ask? To want a guy to take his time with me, make it good for me? Is this it? Does no one know how to fuck anymore? Or is it just that we've all watched too much porn and think that's how it should be? Only it never is, because porn is a fantasy."

Zac took a breath, and Chris was right there with him. But he wasn't finished with the questions.

"So, bit of a more personal question here," Chris began, but Zac cut him off with a snicker.

"I don't think we could get more personal, do you?" He sipped his drink. "What do you wanna know?"

"Forget about it not lasting very long. While they were fucking you, did you enjoy it? Did it feel good?" Chris had a hunch this was key to Zac's dilemma.

Zac stared into his glass. "Not really. Didn't seem to matter if I was topping or bottoming—the result was the same. I kept waiting for that moment they tell you about? You know, when it starts to feel really good?"

"And it didn't come," Chris guessed.

Zac's gaze met his. "No, it didn't. Which kinda told me I need more practice."

It told Chris something else entirely.

"These guys… Can I ask if they were your age? Older? Younger?"

Zac pursed his lips, frowning. "Mostly my age." Chris smiled, and Zac narrowed his gaze. "What?"

Chris gave a casual shrug. "The remedy just seems obvious to me. Stop dicking around with boys, and find yourself a man." Not that he thought Zac would fare any better if he was getting fucked by an older guy, but someone Chris's age and experience would see what Zac apparently could not. And although Chris would *love* to be the one who had Zac writhing on his cock, barely holding on as Chris brought him again and again to the edge, his instincts told him that wasn't what Zac needed.

Then he became aware that Zac had gone quiet.

Zac's lips twitched. "And I suppose *you're* the man who'll put it all right, hmm? Ever thought there's a reason why I haven't been with a guy your age? Maybe because it would feel too much like *fucking my dad*, that's why."

Chris chuckled. "Yeah, I'm not into incest either. But as for me being the one to put it all right…" He locked gazes with Zac, his heartbeat racing a little. "Try me."

Zac swallowed. "You're… you're serious."

Chris nodded, leaning in closer until their faces were inches apart. "Because having someone take their time with you is *not* too much to ask. Because foreplay can last all night long if you want it to. Because I don't need to be inside you to make you come, and if you don't think that's possible, then baby, you really *have* been with the wrong guys." He smiled. "I promise you. When you're shooting your load into my mouth, the last person on your mind will be your dad."

Zac's eyes widened, and his breathing quickened.

"And for your information, fucking is *not* a dying art. You just hadn't met someone who could fuck you the way you need to be fucked. Until now." Except Chris already had a good idea that his idea of fucking might differ widely from Zac's.

You need a mentor. And Chris was determined to step into that role.

Zac's Adam's apple bobbed hard. "And… what proof do you have? That you can do all this?"

Chris didn't hesitate. He cupped the back of Zac's head and pulled him into a kiss, his tongue licking along the seam of Zac's lips, demanding entrance. Zac opened for him with a soft moan, and Chris explored him, rejoicing when Zac's tongue met his and they took the kiss to a new level. Zac's hand was on his shoulder, his scent was in Chris's nostrils, and the bar around them melted away as the kiss deepened.

Then Zac broke away, his chest rising and falling rapidly beneath his dark blue shirt. "Fuck, you can kiss." His pupils were large, his lips slightly swollen.

"I can do other things too," Chris said with a grin. "Now you have to decide if you want to find those out for yourself." He leaned again, until their foreheads touched. "I'll make it good for you," he whispered. "If that's what you want."

"Yeah, it is." Zac's voice was equally quiet.

Chris paused before delivering the bad news. "But not tonight."

Zac jerked his head back. "What the fuck?" He gaped. "You... you kiss me, you get me more worked up that I've ever been—then you pull the plug? What are you, some kind of sadist?"

Out of the mouths of babes. "On occasion," Chris admitted. He didn't want there to be any surprises.

Zac opened his mouth, but no words came out. His pupils, however... The blue was almost obliterated.

Chris had to stifle his own moan. The thought that Zac wasn't completely vanilla was a huge turn-on. Nevertheless, he pushed aside his own needs and focused on Zac's. "I'm not about to just... dive in. I want to take my time with you. I don't want to know what makes your engine tick—I wanna know what makes it *purr*. I wanna watch you, learn what your boundaries are, how far I can push them." He smiled. "And I can't do that in one night. So knowing that, let me ask you again. Is this what you want?"

Zac stared at him, his eyes still wide. "Yes," he said at last. "Just..."

"Just what?" There was something so earnest about him that it tugged at Chris's heart. *Easy now. This is just sex, remember? No boyfriends, no partners, not interested in that? Don't get carried away.*

"Will you make me wait long before we *do* get started?"

Chris wanted to laugh at the difference in him. He cupped Zac's nape. "No, I won't do that. In fact... we can start tonight."

That hitch in Zac's breathing was delightful. "How?"

Chris had the perfect place in mind.

WATCH AND LEARN

"Taking a dick is not the only way to have a good time."

"What is this place?" It had looked like nothing from the outside, just a bar, but now they were inside, Zac was getting a whole different vibe. A darker vibe, that sent a frisson of excitement trickling through him.

"Just a bar where I like to hang out sometimes."

Zac still couldn't believe the turn his night had taken. One minute he was watching the usual parade of guys, mentally assessing them, ticking off the ones he'd already fucked, and dismissing the barely legal guys. The next, he was in a bar that apparently had difficulty paying its electricity bills, judging by the poor lighting, but which seemed to be stuffed to the rafters with men. Mostly bordering-on-naked men.

"And why am I here?" To be honest, he hadn't known what to expect. Chris was like no other guy he'd ever met. He had this cool, relaxed air about him, like nothing fazed him. *Maybe that's what comes with age.* Whatever the reason, Zac liked it.

He liked the way Chris looked too. He was lean, with short dark hair and piercing blue eyes. A tattoo curled over his collar bones, and eagles' wings spread upwards from his wrists to his elbows. Not a drop-dead gorgeous kinda guy, but Zac wasn't interested in someone who could win a beauty pageant. What was between Chris's ears was much more important.

"So I can watch and learn."

Zac was about to respond that Chris could do that anywhere, but the words caught in his throat when the guys around them quietened, and two men got onto the small stage in front of them. They faced each other, both wearing jocks and boots.

"Something tells me they're not about to recite poetry," Zac quipped, but he couldn't tear his gaze away from them. Then one guy sank to his knees, while the other lowered his jock to reveal a stiff, meaty cock. Guy #1 didn't hesitate. He kissed the shaft lightly, letting his lips linger on the head, before taking it into his mouth with a soft moan. Guy #2 smiled, his hands on Guy #1's head, not exerting any pressure, just holding him steady, making soft sounds of pleasure.

And Zac couldn't look away. He watched, mesmerized, as Guy #1 slid his lips along the veiny shaft, taking his time, one hand on Guy #2's ass, the other pulling gently on his sac, playing with his balls.

Then Zac became aware of Chris shifting position to stand behind him, his hands coming forward to rest on Zac's chest.

"What are you—?"

Chris's hand covered his mouth, and Chris whispered in his ear, "Keep watching." Slowly he removed his hand.

Zac did as instructed, shivering when Chris's fingertips brushed against his nipple that pushed at his cotton T-shirt. Then he shivered again when Chris flicked the little bud through the cotton. In front of him, Guy #1 gripped Guy #2's hips with both hands and picked up speed, head bobbing faster as he sucked him off.

"Getting hot in here, isn't it?" Chris's breath tickled his ear.

Zac bobbed his head once, his own breath hitching as Guy #1 swallowed that cock to the root, Guy #2 now exerting pressure, forcing his dick to go deep. When Guy #1 gagged, saliva dripping from his mouth and chin, Zac stifled a groan as Chris slid a hand under his T-shirt to stroke his belly with a firm touch.

"Which would you like to see—him swallow that load or take it in the face?"

Zac moaned at the thought of cum spattering Guy #1's cheeks, nose and chin. "Either," he lied. Then he moaned as Chris reached under his shirt, Zac's T-shirt riding high on his belly as he played with Zac's nipples. Zac arched his back, his cheek coming into contact with Chris's, the rough stubble grazing him.

Guy #2 was driving his cock into Guy #1's mouth, his hips snapping forward as he thrust faster, all the while holding onto Guy #1's head, his fingers wound through the hair. Zac's heartbeat raced and perspiration covered him, cooling his skin as the air hit it.

"Oh, you do like this, don'tcha?"

Zac's intended retort was lost when Chris seized both nipples and tugged hard on them, twisting them slightly. "Oh fuck," he moaned weakly, his knees buckling a little. The combination of the erotic sight before him and Chris's sensual onslaught had him closer to the edge of climax than he would have believed possible.

And he hasn't touched my dick once.

Then all such thoughts fled when Chris's hand covered Zac's throat and he squeezed ever so gently, his fingers still toying with Zac's nipple. "You like this?" Chris sounded breathless, as if he too was close.

Zac managed the tiniest nod, before losing himself in the sight of Guy #2 crying out as he aimed his cock at Guy #1's face and shot hard. Guy #1 opened his mouth like a little bird, his tongue popping out to catch a few drops, before licking his lips, unable to open one eye as it too was coated.

"Fuck, that's hot," Zac whispered, before realizing Chris was rubbing Zack's dick through his jeans. Around them, came soft moans and noises of approval, and Zac caught the tell-tale odor that told him a few guys had just shown their own form of appreciation.

"Do you want to come?" Chris asked him in a whisper.

Zac could only nod, then sighed with satisfaction as Chris used both hands to unfasten his jeans, before licking his palm and slipping his hand into Zac's briefs. He worked the shaft, its head emerging above the waistband as Chris slid his hand faster and faster, tugging hard, until Zac knew he was about to come.

"Now," he managed to croak, as he creamed Chris's fingers. He sagged against Chris's body, grateful for his presence, while his cock pulsed out its last drops. They stood like that for a moment, the music suddenly swelling in volume, as if to cover the backdrop of sounds that was obvious all around them.

Finally, Chris reached into his jeans pocket, removed a handkerchief, and calmly wiped away all traces of Zac's orgasm. He cleaned his hand, folded the handkerchief, and replaced it in his pocket.

Zac didn't wait for words. He spun around, locked his arms round Chris's neck, and kissed him, deeply and fervently, trying to hold onto the glorious feeling that flowed through him. When he eventually broke the kiss, Chris grinned.

"So... I did good?"

Zac shuddered. "I need a drink." Not to mention an explanation. How had a complete stranger seen so much, to have him coming in his hand like that?

Chris nodded. "*Now* we talk."

Zac couldn't stop staring at Chris as they drank their beers. "Okay, you have to tell me your secret. What are you, some kind of sex guru? Is this what you do, go around giving guys the best orgasms of their lives?"

Chris chuckled. "I take it that lit your fuse."

Zac snorted. "Lit it, then sent me into the stratosphere, like there was a rocket up my ass."

Chris nodded knowingly. "And that brings us to the crux of your problem."

Right then, if Chris had said he could spin straw into gold, Zac would have believed him. Instead, he waited.

Chris leaned in close. "What I am about to tell you, is an age-old secret, known only to the wisest of gay men."

Zac nodded eagerly. "Tell me."

Chris's lips brushed Zac's ear, making him shiver. "Some guys just don't get off having a dick up their ass."

He froze. "What. The. Fuck?"

Chris's eyes were bright. "They don't tell you that one, do they? Instead, you get fed a diet of how anal is the be-all end-all of gay sex. The pinnacle to reach. Maybe even have two dicks in your ass at the same time—even better." He sighed. "Meanwhile, there are a lot of men out there who do *not* do anal, for a variety of reasons. Yours happens to be that you just don't like it."

"I don't—" Zac was lost for words.

Chris nodded sympathetically. "I know. You thought there was something wrong with you, or with them. What you lacked was someone to remind you that taking a dick is not the only way to have a good time." He smiled. "And you did have a good time, didn't you?"

Zac laughed. "Like you have to ask." He couldn't remember the last time he'd shot so hard.

"And as for how I knew? That's easy. It's not magic—it's age."

"Age?" Zac frowned. "What's age got to do with it?"

"When you've been around, seen a few things, like I have, there's little that surprises you about sex. And I've met a lot of guys who just don't do anal. The problem is, they're made to feel like they're some kind of anomaly for feeling that way. Like you did." Chris chuckled. "I'm not this all-seeing superman, all right? Although… I did employ a few tricks that I figured might work with you, based on what I'd observed."

"Tricks?"

Chris stilled. "Nipple play. A tiny bit of choking."

Holy fuck. "How… how did you know I'd like those things?" Because up until that point, even Zac hadn't known.

"When you asked me if I was a sadist, and I said on occasion." Chris's eyes darkened. "You might not have uttered a word, but the way you became so still, the way your pupils dilated… That told me what I needed to know."

"And what was that?" Zac's words crept out like a whisper.

"*You* are not totally vanilla, Zac. You like your sex

with a bit of kink. How much kink, I'm not sure right now." Chris chuckled. "At least we know one thing that'll get you off every time."

"We do?"

Chris cupped Zac's chin, and for one moment Zac thought he was about to be kissed. Then Chris gently turned Zac's head toward the stage, which was now bare. Chris's warm breath tickled his neck. "You like to watch."

Zac swallowed. "Doesn't everyone? I mean, what else is porn for, but to be watched?"

Chris shook his head. He let go of Zac's chin. "Porn's not real. You know it, hell, everyone knows it. You really think you're watching two guys going at it for thirty to forty minutes, with no breaks, and all those changes in position? Hell, I've *done* porn, and let me tell you, it can be *the* un-sexiest thing ever. Sure, you can watch a couple of minutes while you bring yourself off, but it's not the same as..."

"As what?" Zac stared at him.

Chris sighed. "Watching two guys—or more— really going for it. Listening to the noises they make. Watching their eyes when they touch each other. Knowing this is real, and hot, and intimate, and taking place *right there* in front of you. Knowing that when they come, there's going to be warmth on their skin, inside them, dripping out of their asses..." He straightened. "There is nothing wrong with watching. And it can be the hottest thing ever."

And that led Zac to The Question of the night. "Are... are we gonna do this again?"

Chris grinned. "Do you want to?"

Zac rolled his eyes. "Duh." Then he thought about it. "But... what exactly will we be doing?"

Chris laughed out loud. "How about you leave that up to me? Just trust me."

That was the strange part. Zac did.

"Is that even gonna fit?"

Chris strolled along Eighth Ave, looking for Zac. They'd agreed to meet outside a restaurant they both knew, because Chris wanted to have a talk with him. There were some things that could *not* be discussed over the phone.

He had to admit, Zac was a breath of fresh air. It was great to meet someone who was so open about their needs and desires, and who actually listened to advice. Too many of the guys Chris ran across thought they knew it all.

The irony of that thought struck him almost instantly. *Isn't that how I must have come across to him last week? Some know-it-all, 'I see right through you' kinda guy?* Well, that was something he had to put right before they went any further.

He spotted Zac at the corner, leaning against the wall, his eyes focused on his phone. Lord, that guy in tight jeans was a beautiful sight. Chris had to give such thoughts a hard push aside. Much as he might want to get into Zac's pants, it wasn't going to happen. And he had to admit that bringing Zac off in that bar had been one of the hottest things he'd done in a long while.

Maybe I should take a dose of my own medicine and stop thinking about where to put my dick.

Zac glanced up as he approached, and he gave Chris a warm, sunny smile. Chris liked the way Zac's hair looked like he'd just got out of bed, sort of tousled and wild. He was wearing a black T-shirt that clung to him like a second skin, his powerful shoulders bare, and the overall effect was luscious.

"Hey." Zac pocketed his phone. "So, what's on the agenda for this evening?"

Chris laughed. "Boy, you're just raring to go, aren't ya? Well, I thought we'd grab a drink here first, and maybe talk over a few things."

Zac arched his eyebrows. "More talk?"

"Put it this way. What I have planned for tonight doesn't happen if we don't talk first."

That did the trick. Zac stood up straight, nodding. "Sure." His manner was suddenly more serious, and Chris regretted his choice of words.

He leaned in and kissed Zac on the cheek. "Remember I said you like your sex with a bit of kink?"

Zac swallowed. "Like I could forget. I... I've been thinking about that all week."

Chris nodded slowly. "Tonight, I'm gonna take you someplace where you'll see a lot of kink, but there are some things we need to discuss first. Kinda like setting boundaries."

Zac was breathing a little easier. "I like the sound of that."

"Good." Chris guided him to the restaurant door. "Then let's get a drink and talk."

Five minutes later they were seated at a table in the window, with two tall glasses containing mojitos in front of them.

"So, where are you taking me?" Zac asked after taking a sip of his cocktail.

"A friend's apartment. It's a party of sorts, except there are no munchies, no booze, just a lot of black vinyl sheets covering everything, some toys, a thumping soundtrack, and a fuckton of lube and condoms for those who want them." He grinned. "Most guys turn up with their own towel."

Zac regarded him thoughtfully. "Doesn't everyone use condoms?"

Chris shook his head. "A lot of these guys are on PrEP. Me included. But I won't be playing tonight." He gave Zac a speculative glance. "I'm not saying everyone should go bareback, okay? But a lot of these guys play together regularly. And you should *always* ask a guy about his status. Not that this is going to matter to you. Tonight, you're just gonna watch and learn."

Zac smiled. "Like you did last week?"

"Exactly. And before we go there, there's one thing we have to talk about. If at any time you decide you don't want to be there, or if anyone asks you to do something you don't want to do? You say Red, and everything stops."

Chris could almost see the layer of calm that settled on Zac. "I like that."

"Now drink up, and I'll take you there."

Zac glanced down at his clothing. "Am I suitably dressed?"

Chris snickered. "I'm not gonna lie. There will be a few naked guys, plus some others in just a jock or a harness. You can keep your clothes on, you can take off your shirt…. Whatever feels right, sweetheart."

Zac drained his glass in three long gulps. "Then what are we waiting for?"

Yeah. Chris really liked Zac.

Then he remembered he had some things to clear up. "Listen, about our conversation last week…. If I gave you the impression that I know everything about you, or that I know what will work for you and what won't, can I just say here and now that that's bullshit? I'm only going on the signals you gave, and—"

Zac pressed two fingers to Chris's lips, and the intimate gesture startled him into silence.

"You saw more in that one meeting than all the guys I've ever been with, so hush." He removed his fingers slowly.

Chris took a deep breath. "Just because I came to the conclusion that you don't do anal, doesn't make it true. If you feel you want to give it another try, then you go ahead. Don't take my word as gospel."

Zac studied him for a moment. "Chris, let me explain where I'm coming from. You promised to make it good for me. You took me to a bar, where I had the most fantastic orgasm I've ever had in my life. As far as I'm concerned, I'm gonna trust what you say. All right?"

"Well, when you put it like that…"

Zac laughed. "So *now* can we go?" He was virtually bouncing on the spot.

Chris couldn't help laughing too. "Come on."

It promised to be an interesting evening.

Zac had that Alice in Wonderland feeling, like he'd landed in a new dimension. Not that *everything* was a total shock. In the intervening week since their first meeting, he'd gone online to take a peek at some BDSM porn. He hadn't mentioned it to Chris, because he had a feeling he knew what Chris's reaction would be. And faced with reality?

Yeah, porn was nothing like it.

The room was exactly as Chris had said it would be, right down to the black vinyl that covered the floor, and the black plastic sheets that covered what few chairs remained. The men who filled the moderately sized apartment were in various states of undress, and Zac spent a moment or two admiring the expanse of flesh. What surprised him was the fact that not all the men there looked like they lived in a gym.

After watching the BDSM porn, Zac shouldn't have been surprised by the large wooden X at the far end of the room, but seeing a guy tied to it, spread out like a starfish, with red welts on his buttocks and shoulders...

Whoa. This was real.

Only, he didn't want to stop and watch. He wanted to see what else lay in store for him. Then Chris tugged on his arm, and his attention was claimed by the metal frame in the corner, from which hung four chains that supported a thin leather base, almost like a hammock but not as long. A naked man lay there, holding onto the chains, his feet in stirrups, his ass hanging over the edge of the leather bed on which he reclined. Three or four men stood around the sling, and Zac was mesmerized by the sounds their slick hands made as they worked their erections, awaiting their turn to plow into the reclining guy's hole.

And Zac wanted to see that.

"Want to get closer?" Chris whispered.

How does he do that? Zac nodded eagerly, and took a step toward the sling, Chris behind him.

The tall man positioned at the reclining guy's ass glanced toward him and grinned. "Watch me slide into him, balls deep. It's sexy as fuck." He aimed his thick bare cock at the bottom's hole, which twitched as if in anticipation. He moaned as Tall Guy thrust into him in one long, strong glide, and Zac wanted to moan along with him at the sight of that glistening shaft disappearing into the dark orifice. He loved how the bottom's body sucked him right in, how he tried to push down on that meaty dick, using the sling to set up the perfect motion as they moved together.

Warm breath whispered against his neck. "Looks good, doesn't it?"

Zac nodded again. When Tall Guy picked up speed and started slamming into the bottom, Zac felt every impact. He might not want to be on the receiving end of that cock, but watching it spear into the bottom's hole was hot.

As if on cue, Chris's hands were on his shoulders, sliding down his bare arms, rubbing and caressing. "Wanna lose the shirt?"

Zac didn't hesitate. "If it means you don't stop touching me? Hell yeah."

A second later, his chest was bare, and Chis was laying soft kisses on his shoulders while he flicked Zac's nipples, over and over again, Zac's gaze focused on that hard dick sawing in and out of the bottom's body. Fuck. It was as if there was a direct connection between Zac's nipples and his dick, and combined with the visuals, he was already looking down the barrel of an approaching orgasm.

"Not yet," Zac whispered, and Chris stroked his chest with gentle hands, caressing his belly.

"How about I show you something else?"

"There's more?" Zac asked breathlessly, his heartbeat pounding. The three men around the sling chuckled at that, and Tall Guy was the loudest.

"Take him into the middle room," he suggested between thrusts. "Tony should be about ready by now."

Chris let out a peal of laughter. "Tony is *always*

ready." His arm at Zac's back, he steered him toward the open door. He leaned in. "Having fun?"

Zac grabbed Chris's hand and brought it down to his solid cock. "What do you think?"

Chris gave it a squeeze. "I think I'm gonna slow things down, because you feel like you're ready to pop." He led Zac into another smaller room, where another sling had been set up, only this time, there were only two men. The bearded guy in the sling had his legs spread wide, his thighs resting against the chains, while the other guy was sitting on a stool between his legs, smearing what looked like white grease over his hands.

He looked up as they approached. "Nice timing. I'm about to give Tony what he's been waiting all week for. Isn't that right?" He addressed the bearded man in the sling, who raised his head and scowled at him.

"Oh, come on, for Christ's sake. I wanna feel ya."

Zac watched as Seated Guy put his fingers together, his thumb tucked in, like a bird's beak, before slowly pushing them into Tony's slick hole. Zac shivered. The most he'd ever been comfortable taking was three fingers, and at this rate, it looked like Seated Guy wasn't going to stop until his whole hand was in there.

Then he realized with a rush of both ice and heat that this was *exactly* what was going to happen.

"Fuck," he said softly. "Is that even gonna fit?"

Chris's chuckle filled his ears. "Trust me, it'll fit. And having a guy's hand inside you? Mind-blowing."

Zac couldn't look away as Seated Guy gently, so gently eased his knuckles through the loosened muscle, until suddenly, his hand disappeared into Tony's body, up to the wrist.

"Holy fuck."

"You got that right," Tony said weakly, his eyes rolling back. "Fuck, it's been too long."

"I got ya, babe," the seated guy reassured him. "Feel me there?" He moved his hand slightly, so slight that it was almost imperceptible, but Tony groaned, and the visceral noise tugged at Zac's insides.

"Ready for more?" Seated Guy asked, and both Tony and Zac moaned.

"I can take a little more," Tony admitted. His fingers tightened around the chains as Seated Guy pushed a little further into him, maybe an inch or so, before slowly withdrawing all the way out of him, leaving his hole gaping, dark red and glistening. This time Seated Guy used his other hand, moving in increments until it too was buried inside Tony's body, his hole stretched tight around the wrist. Seated Guy left it there, at peace inside him, while he dipped his original hand into the white greasy lube.

Chris's lips brushed Zac's ear, and sent a shiver through him. "Watch this."

Zac's gaze was locked onto Seated Guy's hand as he pulled gently out of Tony's body, but before it was completely removed, he pushed in the fingers of his other hand. Slowly, leisurely, he set a rhythm, sliding one hand deep into Tony's rectum, then pulling it out to make space for the other hand, until Zac was certain Tony was about to be stretched wide open by both hands at once.

They never quite got there, but he found himself holding his breath and watching the interplay of the two hands, as Seated Guy enjoyed Tony's body. The noises pouring from Tony's lips grew in volume and frequency, and without laying a finger on his own dick, Tony shot hard, coating his chest and belly in cum, a loud, almost primal cry tumbling from his lips. Seated Guy stilled, waiting for the body tremors to die away, before easing his hand out of Tony's hole. He wiped his hands, then stood up, gently penetrating Tony until his cock was fully sheathed inside him.

Tony let out an obvious sigh of contentment. "God, yeah. I need you."

Chris tugged on Zac's arm. "Let's leave them to it," he said quietly. He led Zac away from the pair and back into the larger room. The guy bound to the wooden X was tilting his hips, clearly demanding to be fucked, his ass bright red.

The man behind him had put aside the whip, and was sliding his slick shaft through the bottom's crack, his hands gripping the guy's hips as he rocked.

"He's been so good, and now he's about to get his reward," Chris said in a low voice. "I think you deserve a reward too." And before Zac could respond, Chris popped the button on Zac's jeans and lowered the zipper.

Zac let out a low moan at the thought of Chris's hand on his dick, but Chris stopped. "Don't tease," he hissed.

"Tell me what you want," Chris demanded. "Do I pull your cock free and make you come, or do I pull your jeans down and try something new?"

That set Zac's heartbeat racing. "Pull 'em down." The demand came out as a whisper.

Chris grabbed the waistband and tugged the jeans lower, over his hips, taking his briefs with them, until they rested around his ankles, rendering Zac naked to all intents and purposes. Chris held out his hand. "Find me some lube."

Zac scanned the space before him and stretched

out a hand to grab a packet of lube, doing his best not to fall over, hobbled as he was by his jeans and underwear. He tore it open and squeezed out the liquid into Chris's palm, then set the packet aside. His heart pounding, he waited to see what Chris did next, his attention torn between the anticipation and the sight of Whip Guy unhurriedly sliding his cock between X Guy's ass cheeks.

"It's hot watching guys getting fucked, isn't it?" Chris whispered.

"Fuck, yeah." There were so many factors that came into play: the sounds; the smell of sex and sweat; the shivers of pleasure that trickled up and down his spine; and the expressions on the guys' faces as they gave themselves up to the sensations.

Then he forgot about the men in front of him as Chris wrapped a slick hand around his dick and he pushed forward with his hips, only to feel a heavy slick dick slide between his cheeks.

Oh my God. Zac was lost.

His world became nothing but that glorious rocking between hand and cock, thrusting through the tunnel of Chris's hand, and feeling a hot, bare shaft move faster and faster, Zac pushing back to feel more of it, both actions interwoven with the sensual moans that came from the men before them.

"Gonna come, sir," the bound man gasped out.

"Oh, fuck, that makes two of us," Zac groaned.

"Then come," Chris demanded. "Come now. Let me feel it all the way through you." He rocked faster, his breathing quickening, his fingers tightening around Zac's dick, tugging hard on it, on his balls, until Zac came with a cry that seemed to come from someplace deep inside him.

When warmth exploded up his back, he knew Chris had come too.

Zac leaned against him, heart hammering, perspiration covering his chest, his dick limp in Chris's hand. "Fuck, that was even better than last time." He turned his head to meet the kiss he knew was waiting for him.

Chris sighed into the kiss. "No arguments here." Then he grimaced. "I think I'd better clean us up before we stick together. Not that wearing my cum doesn't suit you."

Zac smiled. "No argument there."

"And when I'm done, wanna see something else?"

This time Zac grinned. "Does a bear shit in the woods?" He wanted to see a whole lot more before the night was through. He glanced at Chris's crotch, his dick once more out of sight. "How fast can you get it up again?"

Chris arched his eyebrows, his eyes sparkling. "Why, you got plans for it?"

Zac nodded. "I think I'm gonna need my ass decorated with your cum again. If you think you can manage it."

Judging by Chris's smirk, such a thing was entirely possible.

"Are they paddling in what I *think* they're paddling in?

Two weeks.

Nothing from Chris for *two weeks.*

Zac was *not* a happy camper.

His job gave him plenty of time for thinking, and right then, that was *not* a good thing, because he couldn't stop his mind from focusing on his meetings with Chris.

Why hasn't he been in touch? Is there something wrong? Are we done?

Then he reasoned he was overthinking this. After all, he had no clue what Chris did for a living. For all Zac knew, he could have a job that took him all over, and he didn't get to spend too long in NYC.

That was when Zac's situation truly hit home.

I've become invested in a guy I know nothing about. We're basically fuck-buddies, except we don't fuck. And yet I trust him more than any other man I've ever met.

It wasn't as if he wanted a relationship with Chris. At least, not the boyfriend kind of relationship. That wasn't on Zac's agenda, and he didn't think it was on Chris's either. But he definitely wanted to keep Chris in his life.

Friday night loomed, and he wanted more than anything to spend it with Chris. Only, Chris was nowhere to be found.

Of course, there was a solution. Zac could have

called him. What held him back was the idea Chris might see him as needy or clingy. Zac didn't want that.

His phone pinged. Zac glanced at it, then picked it up to stare at the screen.

Got a minute?

Zac pressed Call without a second's hesitation. "I was starting to think you'd left town," he quipped, doing his best to keep his voice even.

"Yeah, sorry about that. Work has been kicking my ass these last two weeks. Plus, I didn't want to talk to you until I had something to discuss."

For a moment, that remark pierced him. *So we can't talk on the phone without having something specific to talk about? Not even as friends?*

Except they *weren't* friends, were they? The only thing connecting them was sex.

That sucked.

"I take it you now have something to tell me." Zac quashed his feelings of disappointment and frustration. Chris wanted to talk to him, so he should quit complaining.

"I know it's short notice, but are you doing anything next weekend? A week on Saturday?"

"Not a thing." In reality, Zac had no idea, but he was pretty sure there was nothing that couldn't be moved if need be.

"Okay. Then how would you like to come with me to a house party in upstate New York? It's being organized by friends of mine, and I think you'd get a lot out of it."

"A house party? As in, staying there for a night?"

"Yup. We'd get there Saturday morning, and the party goes on till Sunday afternoon. And I should say at this point that you'll probably be sharing a room with me. If that's okay."

That was more than okay. "Sure. What about dress?"

Chris snickered. "Casual will do fine. For you, at any rate. You're gonna be dressed, which is more than can be said for most of the guests."

Okay, now he really *had* piqued Zac's interest. "Just what kind of house party is this?"

"I don't want to spoil the surprise. All I *will* say is, keep an open mind." There was a pause. "Okay, I gotta go. Sorry I can't meet up this weekend, but there are things I wanna get done to leave next weekend free. I'll be in touch about getting there, all right?"

"Have a good weekend." Zac finished the call, then stared at the phone.

Keep an open mind? He'd thought fisting and SM were enough of a step outside his comfort zone, but this house party was beginning to sound like they were just child's play in comparison.

Zac couldn't wait.

Their taxi pulled into a long, curved driveway, surrounded by tall trees. Zac couldn't even see any sign of a house. Beside him, Chris sat quietly, hands clasped in his lap, looking cool in a white shirt open at the collar, dark brown pants, and a cream jacket, the picture of summer elegance.

He really is a good-looking man. That five o'clock shadow was sexy as fuck. But for Zac, Chris's best features were his piercing blue eyes. He got the impression Chris saw a *lot*.

"So how do you know these people?" Zac inquired as the taxi pulled up in front of a two-story white house, complete with covered front porch where rocking chairs sat. To the left was a large garage, and there were obviously rooms above that. Dormer windows set into the roof gave the house a charming appearance. Already the gravel space in front of the house was filled with four or five cars, and off to the right was a low stone wall, beyond which Zac got a glimpse of a pond and yet more trees.

"Matt and I go way back. I was his best man when he married Jake. I've been out here a few times since they moved. I think it's the coolest house they've ever had." He grinned. "And I love the pool." He paid the driver, and they got out of the car. Chris pointed back in the direction they'd come. "You know where the driveway forked, and we took a right? Well, if you took the left, you'd end up at their guest cottage. It's fully contained, and not far from the pool house. That's where they're putting us tonight."

"Great." Zac peered up at the house. "This is beautiful. Are there going to be many guests?"

"Maybe fifteen to twenty."

Zac waited, but nothing more was forthcoming. "You're not gonna give any clues as to what I'm gonna find in there, are you?"

Chris simply smiled and rang the doorbell.

He sighed. "All this enigmatic shit is—" Anything else he'd been about to say died in his throat at the sight of the naked man wearing a collar and a metal cage on his dick who opened the door.

Hoo boy.

The man bowed his head. "Welcome, gentlemen. My masters ask that you join them in the garden for drinks." They stepped into the cool interior, and he closed the door behind them. "Please, leave your bags here. I will see that they are taken to the cottage."

Zac and Chris followed him through the house, into a large, airy space filled with comfortable-looking couches and thick rugs, and through that into the covered back porch where doors led to the rear garden.

Zac nudged Chris. "Is this for real?" he whispered. "Do they really have a naked servant?"

Chris's lips brushed his ear. "He's more of a slave, to be honest. And yes, he lives here too. Usually dressed like that."

Zac was stunned into silence.

Chris headed for a tall, distinguished man standing in the middle of the lawn. The man greeted them both with a warm smile. "Chris! It's been way too long. And you must be Zac." All around them stood men of differing heights and builds, drinking what looked like lemonade. Another naked man brought them glasses.

Chris gave the host a hug. "Looking good, Matt. Early retirement obviously agrees with you." His eyes twinkled. "That is, if you really *have* retired."

Matt flushed. "God, you know me too well. I fully intended taking a back seat and letting Jake run the company, but you know me…." He extended a hand to Zac. "It really is good to meet a friend of Chris's. I know you're going to have a lot of fun this weekend."

"That's what Chris says," Zac admitted, shaking Matt's hand. "He just doesn't tell me what that fun will entail." He aimed a mock glare at Chris.

Matt laughed. "Well, let me clarify the main points. You're here as an observer. You are under no obligation to participate." Matt's eyes gleamed. "Unless you want to. You wouldn't be the first guest to change his mind once he got into the swing of things." His face lit up as another man joined them. "Allow me to introduce my husband, Jake."

Zac noticed the age difference immediately. Jake couldn't be more than thirty, whereas Matt had to be in his late forties or early fifties. Jake kissed Matt's cheek, then extended a hand to Zac.

"Glad you could be here." He grinned at Chris. "And you. Where the hell have you been? Please tell me we get to play with you today. It's been too damn long." His gaze flickered to Zac, and his eyes gleamed. "And you, gorgeous. You're included in that invite too."

Zac stiffened, but he needn't have worried. Chris's arm was at his back, a comforting touch. "We're not playing today, Jake."

"Which he knows full well," Matt added. "Jake just can't resist a pretty face, can you?" He gave Chris a knowing smile. "Plus, he's got a thing about that anaconda you keep in your pants. You know Jake and big dicks."

Chris laughed. "The anaconda is in hibernation for now."

Zac was torn between gratitude that Chris had his back, and curiosity. He'd only felt Chris's erect cock in his crack, but now he sure as hell wanted to see it.

Matt glanced at his watch. "If you two go and freshen up, by the time you get back here, we should be ready to start." He addressed the assembled guests. "Gentlemen. It's time."

Chris tugged on Zac's arm. "Come on. Let's do as Matt says."

"You know where we'll be, right?" Jake said with a grin.

Chris waved him off, laughing. They walked back into the house and through it, Zac's mind mulling over what Matt had said.

What in the hell am I going to walk into here?

The gravel crunched beneath their feet as they approached the front door once more, only this time it stood ajar, as though waiting for them. Zac took a deep breath.

"Do I look okay?" He hadn't expected to find a change of clothing laid out for them, especially the leather harness. He had to admit the tight shorts fitted him perfectly, even though they revealed a lot more of his ass than he'd ever shown before. The sleeveless vest showed a lot of his chest, and Chris had made a point of pulling the fabric aside to brush his fingers over Zac's nipple, making him shudder.

But Lord, how Chris looked when he'd emerged from the bathroom…

He wore a snug leather harness, but what got Zac's attention was the mat of hair that covered his broad chest. Zac had an overwhelming urge to rake his fingers through that hair, and he couldn't stop staring.

"You look great," Chris assured him. "You're gonna get a lot of looks, because *baby*, what those shorts do for your ass…."

Zac swallowed, unsure how he felt about strangers ogling his butt.

Chris grabbed his hand and squeezed it. "Remember what I said last time? If it gets too much, just say Red and I'll get you out of there."

"One clue, please?" Zac didn't want it to be too much of a shock to the system.

Chris sighed. "All right then. Most of those guests you saw just now? They are going to be fucking each other's brains out, all over the house, and in many different ways. We are talking a *lot* of sex, and virtually all of it is going to be fucking hot. That's all you need to know." He grinned. "What's your record for the number of orgasms in one day? Because prepare to break it."

Before Zac could think of a single reply, Chris led him by the hand into the house. And before he'd taken as many as five steps into the living area, Zac was sucked down once more into Wonderland.

On one of the couches, two guys were making out, both wearing just shorts, their hands out of sight as they worked each other's dicks. From the eager way they kissed, Zac got the feeling they'd been waiting a while for this encounter. He stood a few feet away, watching them touch and caress each other, loving the soft moans and sensuous noises that poured from them.

"Good start?" Chris asked.

Zac could only nod.

"Then how about we go for a stroll and see what else is going on. Because trust me, these two are going to be the most vanilla thing you'll see here." He led Zac off to the right, into what appeared to be a media room. A huge TV screen dominated the room, but that wasn't what drew Zac's attention. In the far corner, one man was kneeling, naked, while another was slowly and carefully knotting ropes around his body. They worked in silence, and the overall effect was one of peace.

"Have you ever seen Shibari?" Chris asked him.

Zac shook his head, entranced by the rapport between the couple.

"It's truly intricate rope bondage, and it's beautiful to watch. I've seen more than one guy fall asleep while he was being tied up, because it can be really relaxing."

Zac wanted to see more, but the lure of what else awaited them around the next corner was too strong. A thought occurred to him, and he had to say something.

"What about drugs?" Not that he'd seen any drug use, but he needed to know.

"No drugs allowed here," Chris told him. "At least not during the day. You may find guys using a little weed after, while they're chilling out. But the only thing you'll see around here is poppers. Ever used 'em?" When Zac shook his head, Chris smiled. "They come in useful during certain… activities."

Now Zac was dying to know *which* activities.

He followed Chris to the patio doors, and out onto a wooden deck. Four or five guys were congregated around a large paddling pool, like the kind kids played in, only bigger.

A *paddling pool?*

Zac stepped down off the deck and walked over to the group. No one paid him any attention. They were too engrossed in their own activities. He took a step closer.

One guy was on all fours in the pool, while another was fucking him, except…

Zac stilled. The guy fucking him was pissing into the kneeling guy's hole, then aiming his cock and driving it all the way in. A third guy was standing over them, hosing them down with his dick. The last two faced each other, one kneeling, one standing, and the standing guy was pissing all over his playmate, some of which was making its way into his open mouth, clearly on purpose.

Oh my God.

Then Zac peered into the pool, and turned to Chris, stunned. "Are they paddling in what I *think* they're paddling in?"

Chris chuckled. "Welcome to your first piss pool."

Zac was trying to find the words. "Have *you* ever....?"

Chris snickered. "I've been piss-fucked a few times. Not my favorite pastime, I'll be honest, but the guy I was with really got off on it, and that was what mattered at the time." He cocked his head to one side. "Not your thing?"

It was so far from being Zac's thing that he couldn't truly express his feelings without offending the participants. "Not really," he said finally.

Chris bit back a smile. "That's okay. It's not for everyone. But I guarantee you'll find something here that will light that fuse of yours." Then his grin finally materialized. "Oh. If you need to pee? Just go in there, rather than finding a bathroom. That is, if you're up for it...."

Dear Lord.

He held out his hand. "Wanna check out the action at the pool?"

Zac nodded and took Chris's hand.

The pool sounded a safer option than the paddling pool.

"Sweet Jesus, *two* of them?"

Chris was feeling very pleased with himself.

As soon as Matt had called to invite him to the party, he knew inviting Zac along was a foregone conclusion. The event was perfect for him. And the fact that it meant Chris would spend more time with him wasn't to be sniffed at either.

Chris had to admit, he really liked being around Zac. He'd worried at first that the younger man would get the wrong idea, and make assumptions about where these meetings were headed, but thankfully, Zac seemed to have his head screwed on all right. Not that Chris didn't find him attractive. Far from it. But Chris wasn't a relationships kinda guy. He liked things nice and open and fluid, and so far, Zac appeared to be of the same mindset.

Thank God.

But that first night, when Zac had creamed his hand... Fuck, that had been hotter than hell. Chris hoped for an opportunity to witness Zac coming again. And again. Because just *watching* him climax had brought Chris to the edge, and as for the party, sliding his cock through Zac's crease had been pretty damn amazing.

The only issue? Chris had had a taste and he wanted more.

"So let me guess. Swimming pool sex is next?"

Zac's teasing question brought him back into the moment. Chris pointed to the stone steps that led up the hill to the pool.

"Never makes unnecessary assumptions," he said in a mysterious tone, and Zac snickered.

As they crested the hill, there was the pool, all the loungers spread out around it, with deep blue parasols covering some of them. Sure enough, there was activity. In the pool, two guys floated on large inflatable pizza slices, lazily playing with each other's dicks as they moved slowly across the surface of the water.

What caught Chris's eyes, however, were the two men by the wooden fence that separated the pool from the forest that bordered the property. One was naked, kneeling, facing the fence, his hands tied to the top railing. He was blond and slim, his back wide, tapering to a narrow waist before swelling into a truly gorgeous ass. The other was a spectacular specimen of a man, a hot daddy with muscles laid on muscles, wearing a leather kilt. In his hand was a flogger that he wielded with ease, bringing its leather tongues down onto the kneeling guy's shoulders and back. Sometimes they landed with a soft thud, at other times with a whisper as he trailed them over the already reddened skin. The daddy's back glistened with sweat as he worked the flogger, and Chris watched his muscles rippling, how his biceps tightened each time he lifted the flogger high into the air.

The hitch in Zac's breathing told Chris he wasn't the only one to be affected by the scene before them. Chris snuck a peek at him. Zac was rooted to the spot, his gaze fixed on the men, one hand slowly stroking his obvious erection that strained against the tight shorts.

Chris edged in closer. "Want a hand with that?"

Zac turned those pale blue eyes on him, and Chris couldn't miss the hunger there. "Please," he whispered.

Chris popped the button, then lowered the zipper.

"I had something I wanted to do, but you're too hard, so I guess we need to deal with this first." He slipped his hand under the fabric, his fingers meeting hard, hot, silken flesh. Chris curled his fingers around Zac's cock and freed it, pumping it, noting how Zac's hips got into the act. Chris put his arm around Zac's waist to steady him, before finding his own rhythm, using the precum that was already present to slick up the shaft.

"Listen to the sounds he's making," Zac said in a low voice, his gaze locked on the kneeling guy. "Like he wants it so much." He shivered as Chris tightened his grip on his dick, adding his own soft cries of pleasure when Chris picked up a little speed. When the daddy lowered his flogger to the ground and lifted up his kilt, Zac moaned. "Oh, God, he's gonna fuck him."

Sure enough, the daddy grabbed the kneeling guy by the hips, and hoisted his ass up into the air, revealing a black plug in his hole.

"Someone is ready for a fucking," Chris noted, his own breathing quickening as he divided his attention between the daddy with the thick curved cock, and Zac's cut dick that fit perfectly in Chris's hand. He smeared more precum over the rigid shaft, then pumped it, Zac pushing up to meet the motions of his hand.

In front of them, the daddy carefully removed the fat plug, before plunging his meaty cock into the younger man's glistening dark pink hole. His creamy skin glowed in the sunshine, only to be obscured in shadow as the daddy plowed into him, hips snapping, their bodies jolted by the impact.

"Oh, yeah, fuck me, fuck me hard," the blond guy cried out, arching his back. The daddy responded by grabbing him by the shoulders, anchoring himself as he drove his dick deep.

Chris couldn't help noticing how Zac's hips moved in time to the daddy's thrusts, his shivers increasing. When the daddy gave a full body shudder, pulling the guy back onto his cock, Chris knew it was all over. Seconds later, the blond's cum coated the railings, and the older man clung to him, his chest pressed up against the blond man's back.

Chris timed his tugs to match Zac's hips, and it wasn't long before Zac stiffened, shooting his load over the grass. Chris held onto him, feeling the tremors that shook him. He waited until Zac was still once more, then wrapped his arms around Zac's frame and held him upright, kissing him on his neck and cheeks.

Zac looped his arms around Chris's neck and returned the kisses, his cock soft, hanging from his shorts. Chris dropped to his knees and reached into his jeans pocket for the thin piece of leather cord he'd brought along. He tied it around the base of Zac's dick and balls, not too tight, but enough that it would do as a makeshift cock ring when Zac got hard again.

Because Zac *was* going to get hard again, and in a very short space of time. Chris had no doubts about that.

Zac was feeling limp and extremely content. The concept of guys spending a weekend together with the sole purpose of getting their rocks off was certainly new to him, but what surprised him more was that no one minded having observers. Then he thought about it. Watching guys fuck got *his* motor running—why shouldn't some guys get off on the idea of people *watching* them fuck?

Talk about a symbiotic relationship.

"I could do with some water," he said as they left the pool, where the two guys on the inflatables had begun a slow, lazy fuck that looked like heaven.

"Me too. There are bottles of water back at the house." Chris led the way down the steps. "Plus, you'll get to see what else is going on."

Zac laughed. "I doubt I'm gonna see anything that beats the piss pool." He hadn't expected to find the flogging so erotic, but watching how the blond guy reacted to the slightest touch of those soft leather tongues on his flesh… Zac had already made up his mind to ask Chris where they could go on a regular basis to see that taking place. There had to be clubs, right? For God's sake, they lived in New York.

Chris snorted. "Don't be too sure. You haven't seen the playroom yet."

"The—okay, what the hell is the playroom?"

Chris's eyes glittered. "It's where Matt and Jake keep their toys."

Now, *that* got Zac's imagination going. "I wanna see," he demanded.

Chris chuckled. "We've got plenty of time. It's pretty much nonstop fucking all day and night here. Tomorrow is when everyone chills out by the pool."

"Then I don't wanna miss a thing." Zac had no idea when he might get such an opportunity again.

They walked around the back of the house and entered through the rear porch doors. The guys in the piss pool had gone from five to three, and a three-way was in progression.

Zac *really* didn't see the appeal.

Inside the house, the air was cooler. Chris went into the kitchen where bottles of water sat in ice buckets on the counter tops, along with trays of watermelon and mango, strawberries and grapes. He grabbed a couple of bottles, then indicated the staircase on the left of the airy living area. "The playroom is upstairs."

Zac followed him up the wooden stairs to a landing. They stood in a long hallway with many doors leading off it. Chris pointed to one door, and gestured for Zac to enter.

Zac's heartbeat raced a little as he pushed open the door and peeked inside.

Oh Lord.

The far end of the room was covered in shelving, and every shelf had a wide selection of dildos, vibrators and prostate massagers. Then he took a closer look.

"Oh my God, that looks amazing." Some of the dildos were extremely intricate, looking for all the world like sculptures of alien genitalia. Fuck. *What must that feel like when it's inside you?*

Zac knew one thing. He did *not* want to find out.

"Imagine sitting on that monster." Chris pointed to a huge dildo that had to be as thick as a man's arm. "Now *that* would be impressive."

"That's my favorite," came a voice from the opposite corner.

Zac gave a start. He hadn't even noticed the room was occupied.

Two men were on a black sheet, one on his back, pulling his legs up to his chest, his ass in the air, while the other gently eased a thick, cone-shaped dildo into his hole. He beckoned to Zac. "Come and see."

Zac couldn't resist. He crossed the room and knelt

beside the man, who was applying more lube to the ridged silicone cone.

"He's not tried this one before," he said in a low voice, "but when he saw it, he had to have a go." He peered at the prone guy, grinning. "You are *such* a size queen."

"Fuck you," the other guy gritted out. He let out a low, guttural sound as his partner eased a little more of the dildo into his body. "Aw, fuck, yeah."

His partner gently rubbed his belly, his gaze focused on the prone guy's face. "Breathe, babe. Nice and slow, remember?" More gentle rubbing followed, and it seemed to have an effect. The guy taking the dildo relaxed a little, his breathing more even.

Zac was transfixed. Having watched a man's hand get swallowed up should have told him that the dildo was going to fit, but it still seemed such an improbability. "Does it feel good?"

The guy taking the dildo gave a contented sigh. "God, yeah." He closed his eyes, a look of bliss on his face.

His partner chuckled. "You won't get much more out of him. He's always like this when we play with the big toys." He regarded his blissed-out lover with fondness. "Normally he's the most talkative guy on the planet, but like this, he's all, 'No, no, I can't possibly take another inch', I go and slide it in there, and suddenly he's like a limp noodle."

Chris gave a soft tug on his arm. "Ready for more?"

Zac got the message. "Sure." He gave the guy a nod, then followed Chris out of the room. Chris pulled the door gently to after them, and Zac smiled. "Yeah. They don't need anyone but each other right now." He straightened, and met Chris's gaze. "Where next?"

Chris pointed to the open door at the end of the hallway. "The master bedroom."

"Are you sure?" It felt like an invasion of privacy for some reason, which was illogical in a house full of exhibitionist, no-holds-barred fucking.

Chris snickered. "Matt and Jake leave their door open for a reason. I don't think for a second they'll be on their own in there." He led the way to the door, then stood to one side to let Zac enter.

The room was filled with light, due to the large windows that covered one wall, and the space was dominated by a huge bed with a dark wood frame. Carved posts stood at each corner, and on the bed, covered by white sheets, were three men.

Before Zac could notice much more, Chris pointed to the foot of the bed, where there was a couch. "That's for us," he said in a whisper.

Zac went over there and took a seat, Chris following, and found he had the perfect spot to view everything taking place. At that moment, Jake lay on his back, and Matt was stretched out over Jake's lower half, Jake's cock against his chest, while Matt was tongue-fucking the third guy whose knees straddled Jake's chest while Jake sucked his dick. All three men were moving together, a symphony of moans and sighs, then the third guy reached down to cradle Jake's head, lifting it off the pillow, encouraging Jake to take more of his dick. He rocked back and forth, thrusting into Jake's mouth, while Matt spread his cheeks and ate his ass with obvious enjoyment.

Zac was in heaven. He rubbed a slow hand over his crotch, unable to take his eyes off the scene before him. Then he let out a gasp as a warm mouth enclosed his nipple. Chris flicked the hard bud with his tongue, before taking it between his teeth and gently tugging on it.

"Oh, fuck." Zac fumbled with the zipper on his shorts, freed his cock, and got his hand in motion, his senses in overdrive. On the bed, Jake shifted, sitting back against the pillows, while the third guy squatted over him, carefully easing Jake's bare thick dick into his hole, then sinking down on it with a groan. He bounced on it, his weight on his hands, and Zac watched every inch of that cock slide in and out of the guy's body, the shaft glistening with lube.

Chris wrapped his hand around Zac's shaft, not stopping in his adoration of Zac's nipple, and Zac was lost. He lay back against the seat cushions, his gaze locked on the men, acutely aware of Chris's tongue lapping his sensitive nipple, his strong fingers curled around Zac's dick.

Jake supported Third Guy's ass with both hands as he commenced fucking up into him, while Matt kissed the two of them, dividing his time equally.

"Take off your shorts," Chris whispered.

Zac didn't hesitate. He shoved down over his knees, to his ankles, then kicked them off. After a moment's thought, he removed the vest too, until all he wore were his boots. Chris nodded in approval, then took Zac's cock once more in his hand, only now, he kissed Zac's chest, tracing a line between Zac's nipples with his tongue.

Zac caught his breath as Matt shifted on the bed, crouching behind Third Guy, his dick slick with lube. Jake pulled the guy down onto his chest as Matt aimed the head of his cock at the guy's hole.

Zac couldn't tear his gaze away as Matt slowly

pushed, amid a soft chorus of moans of 'oh fuck' from Third Guy, until Matt was buried inside him.

"Sweet Jesus, *two* of them?" Zac's jaw dropped.

"That's a lot of dick we're putting in there," Matt said breathlessly.

"You're not fucking kidding!" Zac said in a low voice, watching as Matt started to move, slowly at first, while Jake remained still, his cock still filling Third Guy.

He noticed everything. The way Jake gently rubbed Third Guy's butt cheeks, spreading him. The way Matt kissed Third Guy's shoulders, keeping up a soft litany of encouragement.

Then Chris shifted off the couch onto his knees between Zac's legs, pushed his thighs apart, and went down on him with a warm, wet mouth.

It was all Zac could do not to explode.

He placed one hand carefully on Chris's head, then focused on the scene on the bed while he pushed up with his hips. The slick sounds that accompanied each glide of Matt's cock into Third Guy's hole were so intensely erotic, that Zac had to breathe deeply to rein in the urge to come. It didn't help that he could hear what the guys were saying, and the dirty talk only ramped up his need.

"Fuck, I can feel your dick coming into his hole," Jake said softly.

Matt slowed down, and Third Guy groaned. "I can feel the end of your cock, that fat head. Feel it when they rub together?" Then Matt sped up, Jake's hands on his thighs, and Jake moaned.

Zac loved how Third Guy kissed Jake, his hands on either side of Jake's head, while Matt thrust faster, their groans mingling. Zac's body tingled, and he held Chris's head firm, his hips in constant motion as his climax approached.

"Fuck, I'm gonna come," Matt gasped. "I'm gonna fucking come so hard in him!"

"Me too," Jake grunted, breaking his kiss. His body became rigid as Matt stiffened too.

Zac made no sound, but shot hard, filling Chris's mouth, shuddering with each pulse from his dick. Chris drank him down, not missing a drop, and Zac cradled Chris's head with both hands, stroking his hair as the final tremors ebbed away. On the bed, the three men held each other, sharing caresses and kisses, but even Zac could see they weren't done yet.

Zac, however, was ready for someone to stick a fork in him.

Chris pulled free of Zac's cock and sat up. Zac couldn't miss the bulge in his jeans, and he leaned forward to run his hand over it.

"Want me to take care of that for you?"

Chris smiled. "Only if you do it in our cottage."

It took a moment for his words to sink in. Zac grinned. "Are you shy about getting your dick sucked in public?"

Chris laughed. "I wasn't shy about coming all over your back, now, was I? Let's just say I'm not in a sharing mood right now."

The thought of having Chris on his back in that big bed, while Zac brought him off with his mouth… Yeah, Zac liked that a lot.

"Then what are we waiting for?"

Chris couldn't hold off his orgasm a second longer. He pushed his head back into the pillows and cried out from the sheer pleasure of it all as Zac swallowed his load, Zac's gentle hands on his belly. The addition of a single finger in his ass had been point of no return, and Chris couldn't recall the last time he'd come so hard. He lay there, enjoying wave upon wave of sexual bliss, until at last he was quiet, his heartbeat returning to normal.

He beckoned to Zac to join him, and in what was a first for them, they cuddled.

"This has been an awesome experience," Zac said softly, his head resting on Chris's shoulder.

"I'm glad." Chris fell silent, enjoying the intimate contact, the scent of Zac, the warmth of his skin against Chris's body.

"But what I want to know is... is that it? Are we done?"

Chris peered at him. "Do you *want* us to be done?"

Zac sat up, gazing at him. "That depends."

"On what?" For the first time, a ripple of unease went through him. He liked things as they were, but what if Zac wanted more than Chris was able to give? Chris didn't want to lose him.

Zac said nothing for a moment, studying Chris in silence. Finally, he sighed. "I like you. I *really* like you. I love what we have. How you see so much of me. And I love what we do. Going to places together... getting off together..." That last remark was accompanied by a smile. "I guess what I need to know is, would you be happy if we continued like that? Sort of... fuck-buddies who don't fuck?"

Chris stared at him. "You don't want a relationship." It wasn't a question.

Zac swallowed. "Not really, no."

Relief flooded through him. "Neither do I."

Zac gaped. "Really? I mean, I know you *said* you don't do relationships, when we first met, but…"

Chris laughed. "What made you think I'd changed my mind?"

That sheepish look was adorable. "The cuddling."

He laughed out loud and held his arms wide. "Come here." Zac rejoined him, snuggling against him. "Okay, confession time. I'm a cuddler. I'm a very tactile person. The main reason you haven't seen that side of me is that I was kinda keeping it in check. I didn't want you to get the wrong idea."

"And the first time we snuggle, I go and get the wrong idea."

Chris chuckled. "We'll put that one down to your age. So… No, I'm not looking for a boyfriend. Yes, I love the idea of having a fuck-buddy. But I'd also like to be able to get to know you better. To have you as a friend too. If that's okay."

Zac craned his neck and beamed at him. "That's totally okay. As long as you think we'll be able to find places to go where we can watch guys."

Chris snorted. "Oh honey. We are *never* gonna be short of those."

Zac settled his head back on Chris's shoulder with a sigh. "Why do I get the feeling that this is the beginning of a beautiful friendship?"

Chris wasn't gonna argue with that.

WATCH AND LEARN

"For me? You shouldn't have."

Four months later

Chris checked the oven. The garlic bread was almost done, and the sauce for the pasta was simmering gently. All that was needed was the birthday boy.

Right on cue, the doorbell rang.

Chris opened it to reveal Zac in his work clothes, his shirt open at the collar and his tie absent, his jacket slung over one shoulder. "Hey, Happy Birthday!"

Zac beamed. "Thanks." He stepped into the apartment and immediately sniffed the air. "Aw. You didn't."

"Why wouldn't I cook your favorite pasta dish on your birthday?" He took Zac's jacket. "I'm not gonna ask how work was. Just sit down, and I'll pour you a glass of wine. Food's ready. And seeing as tomorrow's Saturday, if you want to sleep here tonight, you're welcome. We can go for brunch tomorrow, if you like."

Zac let out a happy sigh. "You know, you'd make someone a wonderful husband."

Chris laughed and ushered him to the table. "Yeah, yeah. You just love me 'cause my cooking beats yours any day." He poured them both a glass of red wine, before going to the stove to add the sauce to the meatballs.

"Hey, where's my present?" Zac called out.

Chris snorted. "You are such a kid." He stirred the sauce, then brought the pan of water up to boiling for the pasta. It wasn't long before bubbling water covered the spaghetti.

Zac appeared in the doorway. "What's wrong with asking? I mean, I got *you* a present on *your* birthday, didn't I?" His eyes glittered with mischief.

Chris speared him with a look. "Yeah, how could I forget? Lemme see, there was a walking stick, a packet of Viagra, a thing for putting on my keys that beeps when I whistle for it, because of course I'm *always* losing my keys... Oh! And a pack of incontinence briefs."

Zac bit his lip. "Well, you *are* getting on, right?"

Chris chuckled. His real present had been tickets to a show that Chris had been *dying* to see, but hadn't been able to get a hold of. "You'd better hope I'm nicer to you, then."

Zac peered around the kitchen. "Then you *have* got me a present."

Chris pointed to the oven. "Seeing as you're here, make yourself useful and get the bread out of the oven. The oven mitts are in their usual place. I'll put out the meatballs."

Minutes later they were both enjoying the fruits of Chris's labor, Zac moaning with pleasure at each mouthful of meatball and garlic bread. Chris loved cooking for him. They tried to have dinner together every couple of weeks, either at his place or Zac's, or someplace downtown. So far, things were working out nicely. They had more in common than Chris had thought, especially when it came to movies, and they often went to the theater.

Of course, there were also those weekends when they went someplace entirely different.

It was the best of both worlds.

Well, *almost* the best, but Chris wasn't going to go there. Not now. Tonight was all about Zac, and definitely *not* the time to confront his own feelings. It wasn't as if he was going to share them, right?

When the meal was over, Zac pushed away his plate with a happy sigh. "That was amazing. I've been looking forward to this all week." He got up from the table, picking up his glass and the bottle. "Couch?"

"Of course." Chris brought his own glass, smiling to himself. He followed Zac to the wide, deep couch covered in pillows. When Zac had settled back against the pillows and kicked off his shoes, his legs stretched out in front of him, Chris reached behind the couch and brought out a gaudily colored bag. "Happy birthday."

Zac's face lit up. "Aw. Thanks." He took it and peered inside, before bursting into laughter. "You couldn't resist, huh?"

"I have no idea what you're talking about." Chris took a sip of wine, trying not to grin.

"Mm-hmm." Zac removed the bright red pacifier, complete with ribbon, and set it aside. Then he took out the pack of Pampers, his lips twitching. Finally he pulled out the knee pads and held them up. "Okay. *This* part, I don't get."

Chris smirked. "Well, you gotta crawl before you can walk, right?"

Zac rolled his eyes. "I wasn't sure if it was some reference to how much time I should be spending on my knees."

"Are we talking about praying?"

Zac grinned. "Well, *some* kind of worship was implied." He put everything back in the bag. "I guess I deserved that." He placed the bag on the floor beside him. "Thanks."

"You're welcome." Chris snuck a peek at his

watch. Almost time.

"What's tonight's movie?" Zac asked, picking up his glass. "You've been all mysterious about it."

"That's because we're not watching a movie tonight. I've got something else planned." Right on time, the doorbell rang.

Zac frowned. "You expecting someone?"

"I'll take care of that." Chris went to the door, opened it, and smiled. "Step this way, gentlemen." The two men standing there looked exactly as they had done online. Perfect. He led them into the apartment, where they stopped in front of Zac, who stared at them in puzzlement.

"Happy birthday, Zac," the taller of the guys said. "I'm Nate, and this is Alex."

"Hi. And thanks." Zac gave Chris an inquiring glance.

Chris gestured to the empty couch that faced Zac. "Over to you, boys."

Nate grinned. "Thanks." He beckoned to Alex, smiling. "Come here." Alex took a step closer to him, until their bodies were almost touching. Nate locked his arms around Alex's neck and kissed him, slow and sensual. Alex responded instantly, the pair of them sinking onto the couch, their hands all over each other, neither paying Zac the slightest attention as clothing was slowly discarded.

Zac let out a contented sigh. He turned to Chris, his eyes shining. "For me? You shouldn't have."

Chris chuckled. "Happy Birthday, sweetheart." He joined Zac on the couch. "Wanna get more comfortable?" From the table drawer, he removed the bottle of lube and a pair of small, clean cloths.

Zac grinned as he popped the button on his pants.

"Don't mind if I do."

Zac tugged on his dick, his gaze riveted on the scene unfolding before him. Alex was on the couch, his legs in the air, and Nate crouched on the rug in front of him, his hands gripping Alex's thighs as he probed Alex's hole with his tongue. Judging by the sounds that poured from Alex's lips, Nate was damn good at rimming.

"Do you like it when a guy rims you?" Chris whispered beside him, pulling on his own thick cock, his jeans around his ankles. Zac loved watching the way his hand moved, varying from slow and sensual, the shaft glistening with lube, to hot and fast, his other hand rolling his balls through his fingers.

Zac snorted. "Never had a guy who spent near enough time with his tongue in my ass. They were always in too much of a hurry to get their dick in there."

Chris sighed. "They didn't know what they were missing. I've had nights when all I did was tongue-fuck a guy, and I lost count of how many times he shot his load."

To Zac's ears, that sounded like heaven.

Nate turned around and grinned at them. "You wanna join us?" He knelt with his back to Alex, his dick pointing toward the ceiling.

Zac stilled. "Excuse me?" Chris's hand froze on his cock.

Alex sat up, his arms around Nate's neck, his hands on Nate's chest. "You two are hot as fuck. And I want to see the rest of you." His eyes glittered. "Because what I see right now is making my mouth water."

"Not to mention making my hole tighten." Nate lowered his gaze to Chris's crotch. "I wanna feel that inside me."

Zac smiled. "Thanks, but I'd rather watch. You're stunning." They both had lean bodies, taut abs, and just the right amount of muscle.

Then he realized Chris hadn't said a word.

Zac glanced at him. "Do *you* want to?"

"Nah, I'm fine." Chris waved at them. "Thanks for the invite, guys, but you're here so the birthday boy can enjoy watching." His Adam's apple bobbed, and his hand resumed its erotic massage of his shaft.

Zac's heartbeat quickened. "And what if I want to watch you fuck?"

Chris jerked his head around so fast, Zac swore he'd get whiplash. "What?"

The more he thought about it, the more Zac liked the idea. "I'm serious. I wouldn't mind watching you with them." *Wouldn't mind?* Zac had no idea how the fuck he managed to sound so goddamn casual, when inside he was buzzing at the idea of watching Chris in action. He cocked his head. "More to the point, I think *you* want that too. You're holding back on my account." He locked gazes with Chris. "You are, aren't you?"

Chris gave a slight shake of his head, clearing his throat, but Zac wasn't convinced.

He leaned in and whispered, "Get your clothes off and get your ass over there. It's my birthday, right? Well, I want this. Don't you disappoint me now."

Chris's breathing hitched, and Zac knew he'd won. Chris kissed him, a fierce, heated kiss that brought a moan to Zac's lips, and then he shucked off his clothing and crossed the floor to where Nate rose to meet him. They kissed, and then Alex pulled him down onto the couch.

Oh my fucking God.

Zac had watched plenty of guys fucking by now, but this was different. This was *Chris* on his knees on the couch, his mouth around Alex's dick, while Nate knelt behind him, spreading his cheeks and burying his face in Chris's crack. These were *Chris's* moans filling the air, *Chris's* head bobbing as he took Alex's cock deep.

Watching guys fuck was always hot.

Watching *Chris* fuck took things to a level of heat Zac had never known existed. He squeezed more lube into his palm and pushed up with his hips, sliding his dick through the funnel of his hand.

At that moment, Chris looked across at him. "Like what you see?" Then a groan fell from his lips as Nate speared Chris's hole with his tongue. "Aw, fuck."

"You have *no* idea." Zac fucking *loved* it.

Nate leaned over, kissing down Chris's spine, and Chris arched, his head back, eyes closed, apparently lost in the sensations. Then Nate kissed Chris's ear. "Do you need a condom? We're on PrEP. Just got the all-clear too, like I said in my text."

"Me too," Chris replied, turning his head to receive Nate's kiss.

"Excellent." Alex grinned and pulled Chris down into a heated kiss.

"Then you're gonna fuck Alex while I fuck you." Nate flickered a glance in Zac's direction. "Wanna watch your boyfriend get his ass pounded?" He handed Chis a bottle of lube.

Zac barely heard him. All that registered was the

fact that Chris was wiping a lube-slick hand over his cock, and he was about to slide it deep into Alex's ass.

For some reason Zac couldn't fathom, he wasn't happy.

Chris grabbed Alex's ankles and spread him wide, while Alex guided Chris's dick into position. "I'm all lubed up and ready to go," he said, gazing up at Chris. "Come on. Want to feel this inside me."

Chris pushed with his hips, moving unhurriedly as he penetrated Alex's ass, and grunted. "Fuck. You're tighter than I expected." He withdrew a little, only to thrust back in, tearing a groan from Alex when he filled him to the hilt. Chris stiffened as Nate mounted Chris, aiming his dick at Chris's hole.

Zac forgot about his dick and focused on the scene in front of him, the three men locked together, Chris shuttling back and forth between hole and cock. The slick sounds should have been erotic, but Zac paid them no mind. He only had eyes for Chris.

Now and again Chris looked over to where Zac sat, his eyes shining as he fucked Alex with abandon, all the while impaling himself on Nate's heavy shaft. Zac wanted to look away, but he didn't. He wanted to blot out the sounds Alex made each time Chris drove his cock deep, but he couldn't. Instead, he remained frozen to the spot, looking on increasingly unhappy as the three men neared the end. When Nate stiffened, digging his fingers into Chris's hips as he shot his load inside him, Zac wanted it to be over.

What he *really* wished was that he'd never agreed to it in the first place.

What he didn't know was why he felt that way.

Chris thanked Alex and Nate as he walked them to the door.

"Anytime," Nate said with a grin. "And thank *you* for joining in."

"Yeah, thanks." Alex leaned in and kissed his cheek. "I really had a good time tonight. So if you ever want to do this again, we'll be here. Just say the word."

Chris watched them head to the elevator, then closed the door. His hole ached, and after the pounding Nate had given him, he was surprised he could walk straight. But he didn't want to think about the sweaty, hot, glorious sex he'd just had.

He had a mystery to solve. *What is wrong with Zac?*

For someone who'd been fired up to watch at the start, Zac was uncharacteristically reticent about the performance. He'd nodded and said all the right things in all the right places, but it was obvious to Chris something was wrong.

And he aimed to find out what exactly was going on.

"So what's changed?"

Chris walked back into his living room. Zac was clicking the lid shut on the bottle of lube, before dropping it into the drawer of the coffee table. He glanced up as Chris entered. "That was some birthday present."

"I thought you might like it." Chris peered at him. "You *did* like it, didn't you?" Because Zac's words weren't exactly effusive thanks, and by now Chris knew Zac well enough to know when he'd really gotten off on something.

"Yeah, it was awesome."

Okay, now Chris was really worried. The *words* were right, but…

"Is anything wrong?"

Zac gave him a wide-eyed stare. "Why should anything be wrong? You cooked a great meal, you invited two hot guys to fuck in front of us… Hell, I even got to watch *you* get fucked. I'd say that is one fantastic way to spend a birthday."

"Do you want to stay?" The thought of sitting with Zac on the couch, maybe watching a movie, seemed the perfect way to end the night.

"If it's all the same to you, I think I'll go back to my place."

"Why?" Chris frowned. "You don't have work tomorrow. And we could do something. Whatever you want." To his own ears, he sounded desperate, and then he realized why.

I don't want him to go.

"I've got a lot of things to do this weekend," Zac explained, "so I wanna wake up early and get started on them. And if I stay here, you'll only distract me." There was the faintest hint of a smile at that point, and Chris's tension eased off a little.

"Okay. Want me to see what we can do next weekend?" Chris didn't doubt for a second that he'd find something they'd both love.

"Sure."

And there was that effusive reaction again—not.

When Zac grabbed his jacket, Chris knew the night was well and truly over. He walked Zac to the door. "I'm glad you had a good time," he said quietly.

Zac smiled. "I had a great time." He leaned in and kissed Chris's cheek. "Bye for now. Have a good weekend." And then he was gone.

Chris closed the door and went back into the living room. He sank onto the couch and stared at the spot Alex and Nate had occupied.

What did I do wrong?

He'd obviously done *something* because the change in Zac had been abrupt. Chris wasn't a stupid man. He knew something had changed in him too.

He's gotten to me.

Four months of being fuck-buddies who didn't fuck, and now Chris wanted more. He couldn't pinpoint the moment when he'd realized Zac had become important to him. Yes, they'd shared some hot experiences, they got each other off while they watched with blowjobs and hand jobs, but that was as far as it went. Zac didn't want more than that.

But now I do.

If he were honest, Chris could admit there had

been changes in his own life. A distinct lack of partners, for one thing, and that had been by choice, not lack of opportunity. Not that he'd shared this with Zac. Because that wasn't them, right? They were just friends.

Except they were more than friends, and he knew it.

We have dinner together. We go to the movies together. We go to clubs and parties together. For two guys who didn't want to be in a relationship, it sure the fuck looked like they were in one.

And then there were the nights when Chris called Zac, just to talk, to hear his voice. They chatted about inconsequential shit, but hearing Zac eased something inside him. It was as if their connection had been re-established. It felt *right*.

Am I so certain he feels like he did all those months ago? Maybe he's changed his mind too. Except if that were the case, Zac would've said something, right?

What, like I've *said something?*

Chris was such a mess.

All of this reflection got him nowhere. Zac had said nothing was wrong. Chris supposed he'd have to believe him, even if his instincts told him Zac was lying his fucking head off. Chris would organize something for the following weekend, and then see how the land lay. If everything seemed back to normal, then fine. If not…

Chris would deal with it.

"Thanks, Matt." The call had made Chris's day.

Matt chuckled. "You're welcome. It'll be good to

see you. And *then* you can tell me why we haven't seen you since the summer."

"I've been… busy?" Chris knew he'd neglected his friends. *I was busy taking care of one friend in particular.*

"Why do I feel you're not telling me something? Whatever. Next weekend, you and I will find a moment for a chat, then you can tell me all about it."

Chris hoped there'd be nothing to tell. He hoped Matt's invitation was just what he and Zac needed to get things back on an even keel. "Sure. Like that's going to be possible. You'll have guests, remember?"

"Hey." Matt's voice softened. "I can always find time for one of my best friends. Especially if he needs to talk."

"Thank you," Chris said sincerely, his throat tightening at the emotion displayed in Matt's words. He disconnected, then sent a text to Zac.

Got a minute?

God, he hoped so. There had been no texts from Zac all week. Okay, he'd replied to Chris's, but with nothing like his usual zingy, witty as fuck responses. These had all been short and sweet.

Sure.

That was all the impetus Chris needed. He pressed Call. When Zac answered, Chris launched instantly. "Hey. I know it's short notice, but do you wanna go to a party Saturday?"

Zac laughed. "Nice to hear you too, Chris. Okay, where is it? And is it the kind of party we'd like?"

"Most definitely. Remember my friends Matt and Jake?"

"Like I could forget that weekend."

Chris chuckled. "It was pretty memorable, huh?" It had also been the catalyst for starting them off on their present journey. "Well, Saturday is their wedding anniversary, and they're inviting a few friends over to help them celebrate."

Zac snickered. "Something tells me we're not talking a drinks-and-munchies kinda party."

"Oh, there'll be those. And black vinyl sheets on the floor, lube in every room, slings—"

"Okay, okay, you've sold me. Sounds great. Will there be as many guests as last time?"

"Matt says not. About ten or so this time." They spent a couple of minutes working out when to meet up at Grand Central, and which train they'd catch, and then Zac had to go because he had a meeting. Chris hung up, relieved.

It's going to be okay. Matt's party was exactly what they needed. A familiar setting, a lot to feast their eyes upon, and multiple opportunities for them both to get off.

Perfect.

It would also provide an opportunity to spend time with Zac, and that was the best part. Chris had missed him. The hardest part of the coming weekend? Not doing or saying anything that gave away how he was feeling.

Zac doesn't want that, remember?

As they stepped into Matt and Jake's house, Zac wondered briefly what he was letting himself in for this time. After all the sights of the previous party, he didn't think there was anything left to surprise him.

"At least it's too damn cold for the paddling pool

this time," Chris murmured as they handed their coats to the naked slave with the collar.

Zac shuddered. "And I *still* don't wanna try that." He glanced at the empty living room ahead of them. "I know you said there would be fewer guys here than last time, but..."

The slave coughed. "Sir, you'll find most of the guests are upstairs in the master bedroom."

Chris grinned. "Thank you." When the slave walked off, he leaned in toward Zac. "Wanna watch your first gangbang?"

Okay. Scratch that last thought about nothing left to surprise me. "Seriously?" Zac stilled. "*Just* watch?" After his birthday surprise, he no longer knew what to expect. *Will Chris want to join in?*

Chris kissed his cheek. "I'm going to be the one with my hand in your jeans, stroking your dick while you watch Jake getting fucked."

Okay, that answered *that* question. "How do you know Jake is the one who's bottoming?"

Chris laughed. "Trust me. I speak from experience." He led Zac up the stairs and along the hallway to the master bedroom. As they neared the open doorway, Zac couldn't miss the groans and grunts that emanated from it. They went into the room, and the smell of sweat and cum hit Zac immediately. There were eight naked men in the room: Jake was in the middle of the bed on all fours, one guy kneeling in front of him, and another behind, and he was being filled from both ends. Four men stood around the bed, watching and working their dicks. Judging by the moans that poured out of Jake, he was loving every second of it. The guy fucking his ass stiffened, crying out as he shot deep inside Jake, and even as he pulled out, another guy took his place.

Matt sat on the couch at the foot of the bed, watching the proceedings, his shaft slick as he slowly slid his hand along it. He glanced up and smiled at Chris and Zac. "Hey. Just in time for the finale." He inclined his head toward the empty space next to him on the couch. "Take a seat."

Zac joined him, and Chris stood at his side. "What's the finale?"

Matt chuckled. "Jake's taken every dick so far, some of them twice. I've lost count of how many loads he'd had pumped into him. But now we get to his favorite part."

Zac was dying to ask why Matt wasn't on the bed with his husband, taking part in the proceedings, but that seemed rude. Instead, he gave the bed his full attention.

One of the guys on the periphery got onto the bed and lay down, his heavy cock standing at attention. Jake straddled it in reverse cowboy, slowly sinking down onto it until he was fully seated. Then the guy bent his legs, tilting his hips, and eased Jake to lie down on his back, his hands grabbing Jake's knees and pulling them up toward his chest.

Another guy got onto the bed and knelt between the bottom guy's legs, his thick, veiny dick slick with lube. He aimed and pushed so, so carefully, and Jake groaned.

"Fuck, that feels huge." He turned his head toward Matt. "Aw, fuck, babe."

"You look amazing," Matt told him, his hand moving faster on his cock.

Zac had never seen anything like it. It wasn't the double penetration that made his breathing quicken, but the sight of all those men, and Jake just taking them all. He popped the button on his jeans and pushed them down to his knees, his dick rising into the air, already stiff.

"Want some help with that?" Chris murmured, grabbing a packet of lube from a nearby table and tearing it open.

Zac nodded eagerly, and Chris wrapped a slick hand around his thickening shaft. Zac focused on the group on the bed, his hips pushing up to meet Chris's hand, making his cock slide through Chris's fingers. Jake was staring wide-eyed at the guy fucking him, who picked up speed, while all around them, the spectators jerked off, their bodies glistening with sweat. Perspiration coated Jake's chest and abs, his arms around the neck of the guy fucking him with long strokes now.

"Oh, oh fuck, oh fuck." When cum pulsed from Jake's dick, one of the watchers got onto the bed and took Jake into his mouth, drinking down every last drop. Tremors coursed through Jake's body, and his moans increased.

"Ready for my load?" the guy on top demanded.

"Ready for mine?" Zac said with a groan, and Chris scrambled to kneel beside him, leaning over just in time to swallow his load. Zac closed his eyes to the scene and lost himself to the sensations: Chris's mouth on his dick, warm and wet; the moans and grunts from the bed; and the smell of Matt's spunk as he too came with a cry.

The only guy not to come was Chris.

Shaking, Zac stroked Chris's head as he rode out the last waves of sensual pleasure. "That was one helluva way to start a party," he murmured. He opened his eyes and gazed at Chris as he leisurely cleaned Zac's cock with his tongue.

"The night is still young," Matt said beside him, his lean torso spattered with cum. He got up from the couch and walked over to the bed. "Gentlemen, I believe it's my turn."

The onlookers stepped away from the bed as Matt climbed onto it and stretched out beside a thoroughly spent Jake, holding him and kissing him, Jake's arms around him. Soft murmurs escaped Matt's lips as he told Jake how amazing he'd looked—and how much he loved him.

Zac stared at them, marveling at how they apparently shut out the world, lost in a bubble of time and space that was just the two of them.

Chris cleared his throat. "That's our cue to leave too," he said in a low voice.

Zac nodded, and pulled up his jeans. He got up and followed Chris from the room, following the troop of naked, sweaty men who were laughing and talking about the experience. Everyone went downstairs and into the kitchen where a bar had been set up, and the middle island had been prepared with trays of snacks and fruit. Bottles of water lined the countertop, and Chris grabbed two of them.

"Come with me." He led Zac through the living room and into the covered back porch, where two couches faced each other. Chris sat on one of them and tugged Zac down beside him. He handed Zac a bottle, and Zac drank greedily. It had been very warm in the bedroom, and he wasn't surprised the participants had been covered in sweat.

"So, how was it?" Chris asked.

Zac thought for a moment. "It looked…" He

struggled to find the right words. Hot didn't even come close. "I liked it," he said simply. He couldn't even *begin* to understand how it must have felt to be Jake, being fucked by so many men, used like he was their plaything. And as for that scene at the end, Jake and Matt, locked in each other's arms…

That one moment had touched Zac someplace deep inside him. *They love each other.* There was no denying that. One glance at their faces was enough. *How easy it must be, to let yourself go, to let your emotions show like that.*

Zac was getting tired of hiding his. *This is no way to live.* And he wasn't sure how much longer he could keep up the pretense before he cracked.

The door from the living room opened, and one of the men from upstairs stepped onto the back porch, now wearing a jock. "Chris. How are you?"

Chris got to his feet and gave the man a hug. "Simon, so good to see you. It's been so long. I'm great." He freed Simon and gestured to Zac. "This is my friend, Zac."

Simon gave him a warm smile. "Any friend of Chris's…" He grinned and gave Chris a mock punch to the arm. "We've missed you at the club." Simon reached down and cupped Chris's crotch, giving it a squeeze. "I've definitely missed *this*. I was hoping you'd join in upstairs."

Chris laughed. "Sorry to disappoint you."

Simon gazed at Zac with gleaming eyes. "And why has he never brought *you* to the club, cutie?"

Before Zac could utter a word, Chris interjected, "Zac likes to watch."

"Then definitely bring him along. He can watch you fucking my brains out. And of course the guys waiting in line to be next." Simon chuckled. "Watching you in action is hot as fuck."

"Simon?" someone called from inside.

Simon nodded toward Zac. "Excuse me." He gave Chris a peck on the cheek. "And you? Get your gorgeous ass back to the club." Then he went indoors.

"A friend of yours, I take it," Zac said after a moment of silence.

"I've known Simon for years. We met at a BDSM club."

Zac nodded, his throat tight. "You know what? I think I need some air. I'll be back in a sec." And without waiting for Chris to respond, he walked into the house, over to the hook where the slave had hung their coats, grabbed his, and headed out the door into the chill night air.

He didn't need air. He needed to think, and he couldn't do that with Chris next to him.

Because Chris was the one confusing him all to hell.

WATCH AND LEARN

"You need to talk."

Zac's feet crunched on the gravel as he walked over to the low wall that overlooked the pond. He wrapped his coat around him and sat on it, staring out at the moonlit water, its surface marred by ripples that spread out across it.

He knew exactly what had brought an abrupt end to his pleasurable evening—Simon. Not that Zac had anything against him personally—Simon seemed like an okay guy, based on that brief encounter—but there had been the implication that Chris had a whole other sex life that Zac knew nothing about.

As to *why* this should burn him…

The door opened and a burst of music drifted out into the night. Zac tensed, expecting Chris to join him.

Zac wasn't ready to talk to Chris.

"Hey. Can I join you?" It was Jake, bundled up in a thick coat, and carrying a packet of cigarettes.

"Sure. It's your wall," Zac joked. Jake sat beside him and offered the open packet. Zac shook his head. "I don't, thanks, but you go ahead."

Jake lit up and took a long drag. He exhaled, staring out over the moonlit pond. "I feel wrung out."

"I'm not surprised."

Jake chuckled. "I had no idea Matt had planned that." He turned his head to look at Zac. "Did it make for a good show?"

Zac let out a long breath. "It was… mind-blowing. You must be sore."

Jake laughed. "There'll be a long, hot soak in the tub before bed for me. That'll help. But yeah, my ass is gonna be out of action for a day or two." He frowned. "Now can I ask what you're doing out here in the cold? And why you're not in there with Chris."

"I just needed some alone time, that's all."

Jake stilled. "And I'm disturbing you. I'll leave you to your—"

"No, don't go!" The plea came out more forcefully that Zac had intended.

Jake swung one leg over to straddle the wall, facing Zac. "I take it alone time means time without Chris." He cocked his head as he took another drag. "Wanna talk about it?"

Zac shrugged. "I hardly know you."

"And yet you sat in my bedroom, watching me get fucked by six guys."

"When you put it like that…" Zac took a deep breath and started at the beginning: meeting Chris in the bar, that first club, the subsequent events… He told Jake about his birthday night, and Chris accepting the invitation. "That was when things changed."

Jake nodded. "So you didn't like watching him fucking with them? Is that it?"

"No, that's *not* it. Watching him was… hot as fuck. It really was. I think I started feeling uncomfortable when Chris told them he was on PrEP."

"Didn't you know?"

"Yes! That's what so weird. He *told* me, right before we went to my first sex party."

"Then what's wrong?" Jake gestured toward the house. "Virtually all the guys in there are on it. I'm on it. So is Matt."

Zac thought about it. "I think what it comes down

to is… he's on PrEP because he's sexually active."

"And there's something wrong with that?" Jake took another drag and flung out his arm. "There's this little thing lurking out there that you might have heard of. It's called HIV. Now, I don't mean to trivialize it, but if Chris is taking precautions, that's a good thing, isn't it? He's taking care of you."

"He's not fucking *me*!" Zac retorted, louder than he'd wanted to.

Jake nodded slowly. "But he's screwing other guys… and that bothers you."

"I don't *know* if he's fooling around with other guys," Zac said helplessly.

Jake stubbed out his butt on the ground. "Okay, let's see if I've got this. You two are friends."

"Yes."

"You're not in a relationship, but you get off watching guys getting off, with blowjobs and hand jobs thrown in."

"Yes."

Jake's eyes locked on his. "You agreed to be exclusive."

"What?"

"You agreed to not see other guys while you're friends."

"Well… no."

Jake was so still. "Sounds to me like something has changed. Do you want him to be *more* than a friend?"

"He doesn't want that."

"How do you know? Have you even asked him?" When Zac's mouth fell open, Jake raised his eyes heavenward. "Christ. Typical guy. Do you know how long it's taken me to *train* Matt to talk to me when he's got something on his mind? He used to shut himself off, shut me out, not tell me what was wrong… And all the time, we could've been spared all that heartache and angst if he'd just sat me down and *talked* to me. Why are guys so freaking lousy at communication?" He speared Zac with an intense gaze. "And don't think I didn't notice you ducking the question. I asked if *you* want him to be more than a friend, and you told me how *he* wouldn't want that."

"Okay, okay, so I *do* want that." Zac sighed. "You're saying I should just tell him what I'm feeling?"

"Duh." Jake removed another cigarette and lit it. "Okay. You need to talk to Chris. You need to tell him your feelings have changed—" He paused. "You're falling for him, aren't you?"

Zac stared at him. "I…"

Jake smiled. "I hate to tell you this, but eating together? Movies together? Sexy dates together to watch guys fuck? That's a relationship. And if you've developed feelings for him, Chris needs to know that. And then you both have decide on some really important stuff."

"Such as what?" Zac's head was still spinning from the idea that a relationship had sort of snuck up on them—and they hadn't noticed. *Talk about being blind…*

"You both need to be very clear about what you want out of this. Specifically, monogamy or… something more open."

Zac swallowed. "Can I ask you something? How do you do it? The open relationship part…"

Jake exhaled. "I love Matt. He loves me. We enjoy playing with other guys and it works out very well. Some of those men in the house come here on a regular basis, because they… enrich what we have. They fill in the gaps."

"What do you mean?"

Jake smiled. "Matt likes to be fisted now and again. Now, I love him heart, body and soul, but I can't do that for him. But our friend Mike? Fuck, he loves it." Jake grinned. "He's been using Matt as a hand puppet for years."

Zac burst into laughter. "Oh my God. Now I can't unsee that."

Jake chuckled. "I know, right?"

"What about you? Are there things Matt can't provide?"

Jake nodded. "I like taking two dicks. And now and then I love being the play toy of a group of men."

"Matt doesn't mind?" Zac recalled the way Matt had watched the proceedings, so focused on Jake.

Jake laughed. "Mind? He thinks it's hot. It's a win-win. He gets to watch me have a good time and get a sore ass. *I* get to listen to the noises he makes when Mike's got most of his arm wedged in Matt's rectum. And when it's over, I'm the one who holds him."

"Like he held you tonight."

Jake nodded. "Which brings us to you."

"What about me?"

"You don't like anal. Nothing wrong with that. Chris does, however. That gives you two options. One, you can suggest you become exclusive, if he feels he can do without the anal part. Or two, you both acknowledge the obvious—you are *way* more than just friends, but you're okay with bringing others into the relationship to provide what you can't." Another tilt of his head. "Is there something you need that Chris can't provide?" Jake's eyes glittered in the moonlight. "Some deep, dark need you haven't even dared mention because you think he'd say no?"

Zac chuckled. "Sorry to disappoint you, but no. I... I just want him to be happy."

"But *you* need to be happy too," Jake remonstrated. "You both need to sit down, talk things through, and come up with a way that works for you."

Zac bit his lip. "There *is* something..."

Jake grinned. "I knew it."

"But it's not like that. When I was watching him with Nate and Alex... Nate was rimming him, and Chris said something about making a guy come with just his tongue in the guy's ass. I... I want that. And..."

"Go on, spill. You've gotten this far."

"Frotting," Zac said quickly. "I've seen it online, but I've never experienced it."

"Why haven't you told Chris?"

"Because it felt too... intimate." A step beyond blowjobs and hand jobs that Zac wasn't prepared to ask for.

Jake sighed. "You know the cottage you stayed in last time? It's yours for tonight. Go there. I'll send Chris to you. Because there's no time like the present." He leaned in and kissed Zac's cheek. "And I hope it works out." He got to his feet. "And now that my ass is numb, I'm going inside for that bath. With any luck, Matt will be joining me." He grinned. "Thankfully the tub will only take two, so I'll have him all to myself. Our guests will take care of themselves. They usually do." He patted Zac's cheek. "Do me a favor? Whatever happens with Chris, will you stay in touch? I'd really like to know you better. You're a sweet guy."

"I'd like that too."

Jake gestured to the golf buggy that was parked near the garage. "Take that up to the cottage. The key's in the ignition. Yes, I know it's not far, but it's dark and there could be creatures lurking in the forest."

"Won't Chris need it too?"

Jake snorted. "Chris is big enough to take care of himself." And with that, he went into the house.

Zac went over to the buggy and headed toward the cottage, his mind going over the conversation.

I guess I need to be clear about what I want.

God, he hoped he and Chris were on the same page.

Chris glanced toward the front door. *I should go find him.* His stomach had been in knots ever since Zac had walked out of the house. Chris was in no doubt that Zac didn't need air, but he clearly needed some space, and Chris respected that.

It didn't stop him from wondering what the fuck was going on, however.

Matt stepped out onto the back porch. "Where's your other half? And why do you look like someone's just drowned your puppy?" He wore a bathrobe, his feet bare.

Chris blinked. "That bad?"

Matt sat beside him on the couch. "You don't appear to be having fun, that's for damn sure."

Chris sighed. "No, I'm not."

Matt patted his knee. "Okay. Tell your Uncle Matt *all* about it."

Despite his overtaxed brain, Chris guffawed. "*Uncle* Matt? Do I have to remind you of our history? Because that makes you being an uncle kind of incestuous."

Matt laughed. "Okay. Tell your *friend* what's worrying you."

"I think Zac is having second thoughts."

"About what?"

"Doing what we do. The clubs. The parties. Getting off together."

Matt shrugged. "Didn't seem that way to me, but then again, I don't know him as well as you do." He peered closely at Chris. "Maybe Zac's not the only one having second thoughts."

Chris stiffened. "What do you mean?"

"This friends-with-benefits arrangement you two have. Is that all it is? Or has something changed?" His eyes widened. "Or do you *want* it to change? That's it, isn't it?"

Chris let out a sigh. "When we started out, I was so sure of myself. I didn't do relationships. I told Zac the night we met that there were no boyfriends, no partners, that all I was interested in was a good time."

"And now?"

"Now?" Chris leaned forward, hands clasped between his knees. "Now I look forward to seeing him. I plan a dinner for us, making sure to cook him something I know he'll love. I love it when we go to the movies, but what I've realized lately is that the best part is sitting there in the dark, so close to him that I can smell his cologne. I love watching him come."

Matt let out a wry chuckle. "For a man who doesn't do relationships, you're doing an awfully good act of being in one."

"But it was so simple when we started!"

Matt nodded. "And now, as it says on my Facebook profile, it's complicated. Have you told Zac any of this?"

"No. I didn't know how to bring it up." Except that was a lie. He didn't want to hear Zac tell him he'd had enough. That he regretted their…

Chris stilled. "Oh my God. You're right. I'm in a relationship."

Matt laughed. "At last, a breakthrough." He put his hand on Chris's back. "Shall I tell you what being with Jake has taught me? The secret to our enduring love affair?"

Chris chuckled. "Do I want to hear this?"

"Maybe not *want*, but you *need* to hear it. We talk. We talk about everything. No secrets—well, we still have some, but those are things like surprises and presents. If something bothers either one of us, we talk it through." Matt shook his head. "He's better at it than I am, but he says I'm improving." He smiled. "See? You can teach an old dog new tricks. And now, old dog, you need to go find that man of yours, and talk to him. Be honest about how you feel."

"You may find he surprises you," Jake said as he joined them, removing a coat. "You'll find him up at the cottage." He grinned. "We don't want to see you until breakfast."

"Call us if you need anything," Matt added.

All Chris needed right then was Zac.

"Can we talk?

Chris pushed open the cottage door and stepped into the warm interior. "You in here?"

Zac's chuckle came from the bedroom. "No. This is a recording."

The door was open, so Chris entered the room. Zac sat on the bed, propped up by pillows, legs stretched out in front of him, crossed at the ankles.

"Hey. Jake said I'd find you here."

Zac nodded. "Could you get me a glass of water from the kitchen?"

"Sure." Chris went into the small kitchen area and found a couple of glasses. He filled them and took them through to the bedroom. He placed them on the nightstand, then sat on the edge of the bed. He watched as Zac took a long drink, but as soon as he'd replaced the glass, Chris couldn't wait any longer.

"Can we talk?" The words came out simultaneously, and they laughed.

"You go first," Chris suggested.

"No, you can." Chris gave him a mock glare, and Zac nodded quickly. "Okay, I'll go first." He took a deep breath. "I'm sorry. There's something I should have said before now, only I didn't know how to begin. And I didn't know how you'd take it."

Chris sighed. "What went wrong?"

Zac blinked. "You felt that too, huh?"

"I knew there was something. But when I asked and you said everything was fine... I should've pushed."

"I'm glad you didn't," Zac confessed. "Because it took me until just a short while ago to realize exactly what was niggling me."

"Then tell me." Chris reached for Zac's hand, and Zac gave it. "I need to hear it, whatever it is."

Zac swallowed hard. "When we first met, you told me you were on PrEP, remember?" Chris nodded. "And that was fine," Zac continued. "Until you mentioned it again that night of my birthday. When you were with Nate and Alex." He paused. "*Then* I had a problem with it."

Something rolled over in Chris's stomach. "You were jealous? But... why? We never said we were exclusive."

"I know!" Zac's eyes were wide. "Watching you fuck Alex wasn't the problem—that was hot, and I fucking loved it. No, what started off this whole mess in my head was…. How do I put this?" Another deep breath. "You fucking guys while I'm there? No problem. But you fucking guys that I don't *know* about? That's a whole different story." Before Chris could tell him how wrong he was, Zac blurted out, "Thinking that you're fucking someone without me? That would eat me alive. I know I can't give you what those guys could. And I know you'd never ask me to. But…" He shuddered. "What it all boils down to is, I don't mind if you fuck someone, as long as I'm there. And I know it sounds illogical, but I can't help it. That's just the way I feel." He bowed his head.

"Zac," Chris said softly. When Zac didn't respond, Chris gently lifted his chin with his fingers, and looked him in the eye. "Zac. That night with Alex and Nate… That was the first time in a while that I'd been with anyone."

"What's *a while*?"

Chris chuckled. "Try four months."

Zac froze. "Really? Why?"

"You'll laugh."

"Try me."

"It felt wrong… because you weren't there." When Zac gaped at him, Chris nodded. "I know. It didn't make any sense to me either. We weren't dating. We weren't even fucking. But it felt like doing that would hurt you… and I didn't want to do that." The tightness in his chest eased, and that flutter in his belly subsided.

"Are we saying… we're in a relationship?" Zac asked quietly.

Chris laughed. "I think we already were. We just hadn't noticed."

Zac's eyes sparkled. "Is this where you kiss me?"

Chris curved his hand around Zac's cheek. "No, this is where I tell you how much you've come to mean to me. How much I love having you in my life. How much I love what we have together." He smiled. "*Then* I kiss you." He leaned in and took Zac's mouth in a gentle kiss, sighing as Zac scooched closer and locked his arms around Chris's neck, deepening the kiss.

Then Zac broke it and pulled back. "Wait a minute. You distracted me."

"I distracted *you*? Who asked to be kissed in the first place?"

"We're not done talking. And this is the important bit," Zac protested.

"More important than finding out we're more than friends?" Chris teased. He knew what was coming, and he was glad of it.

Zac let out a quiet *oh*, and Chris suddenly had his

arms full, warm lips against his, and a warm body pressed up to him. "Have I ever told you what a great kisser you are?" Zac murmured.

Chris chuckled. "The night we met. Now, let's talk."

With obvious reluctance, Zac sat back against the pillows. "So it's official. We're in a relationship."

"Agreed."

"An open relationship?"

Chris had to know. "Are you really okay with that?"

Zac stroked his chin. "Are you asking me if I want us to play with other guys, and if I want to see you getting fucked?" He grinned. "Hell yeah."

"And if guys want to play with *you*, or you with them?" Zac smirked, and Chris gave him a speculative glance. "What just crossed your mind?"

"I was thinking about the noises you made when Nate was eating your ass. I think I need to see if he's as good at it as I think he is." Zac's smirk gave way to a grin.

Chris laughed. Lightness stole over him, filling him, and for the first time in at least a month, he felt happier about their future. Because now they had one— together.

"So… we play with others, but only when we're together," he said.

Zac nodded. "Agreed."

Chris stroked his cheek. "So you need never worry about me being with someone else while you're not there," he said in a low voice.

Zac's smile reached his eyes. "Yeah." He shifted closer, and Chris breathed him in, loving the way Zac's scent stirred him. Their mouths met, and Chris let go, kissing Zac how he'd longed to kiss him for so long, murmuring against his lips how beautiful he was, how special. Zac's soft *oh* and the way he deepened the kiss were oil on the troubled waters of Chris's soul.

He's mine.

"Do we need to go back to the party?" Zac said quietly, his face buried in Chris's neck.

Chris pretended to consider the question. "We *could*… or we could stay here, and I could give you something to compare Nate's skills with." The thought of getting his tongue on Zac's hole flooded his mouth with saliva, and his fingers ached to feel that soft, warm flesh as he parted those downy cheeks to reveal his prize. His heart pounded. This was new.

Oh my God. The look in Zac's eyes, the delicious hitch in his breathing… "Won't we be missed?"

Chris snorted. "Hell no."

"In that case, I think I like the sound of that."

"You're sure?" Chris wasn't going to make a move until he was certain this was what Zac wanted.

Zac slowly reached down to grasp the hem of his sweater, then leisurely pulled it up and over his head, revealing bare skin. Then he freed the button on his jeans, pushing them down over his hips, his knees, struggling a little near the end because they were so tight. Chris got in on the act, tugging them off, until Zac was naked on the bed, his dick as hard as it had been during the gangbang. He pulled slowly on his cock, his gaze locked on Chris.

"Does this look like I'm sure?"

Chris squirmed out of his clothing, tossing it aside on the rug beside the bed, then stood beside the bed, his own cock rising at the sight of Zac's obvious arousal.

Zac grinned. "I'm guessing that's a yes."

Chris clambered onto the soft comforter. "Face down," he instructed.

Zac's eyes widened briefly, and then he flipped over onto his belly, tilting his ass, presenting it to Chris. "Ready."

Chris crawled up Zac's body, making sure to drag his heavy cock through Zac's crease, eliciting a moan. He kissed Zac's shoulders. "Has no one ever tongue-fucked this beautiful ass?" He reached down to grab one plump ass cheek and squeezed it.

Zac turned his head to the side, looking at him. "Uh-uh." He caught his breath as Chris slid a single finger through his crack and rubbed over his hole. "That feels good," he whispered. "But you're not gonna—"

Chris stopped his words with a kiss. "I'm not stupid," he murmured as he drew back. "Just because one important thing has changed between us, doesn't mean you've suddenly developed a hankering to be fucked." He chuckled. "My dick may be a lot of things, but magical isn't one of them."

Zac shuddered, and Chris knew instinctively he'd said the right thing. "Spread for me," Chris whispered. "As wide as you can."

"Oh fuck." Zac spread his legs, and Chris got his first look at that tight little hole.

"That's so pretty." He languidly licked down from Zac's tailbone, dragging his tongue over Zac's pucker, and Zac shivered, his hole contracting. Chris did it again, and Zac moaned. "You like that."

Zac contorted his body until he was staring right at Chris. "Did I say you could stop?"

"Oh, yes, sir. Sorry, sir." Chris chuckled as he

resumed his licking, a casual, leisurely trace of his tongue through Zac's crease, pausing to circle the ring of tight muscle, then continuing on his way, down over his balls and right to the end of his dick, resting against Chris's palm. Then he changed direction and licked his way back up, dragging over Zac's ball sac and pausing yet again at his hole. Only this time, Zac rocked, his ass bobbing up and down, Chris's tongue sliding over the ever-loosening pucker again and again.

That was the cue Chris needed. He grabbed Zac's cheeks and pulled them apart, stretching his hole wide. Then he probed Zac's entrance with his tongue. *Circle, lick, push, circle, lick, push…*

Zac reached back and grabbed his head. "Fuck, oh fuck, don't fucking stop."

Chris had no intention of stopping. The goal was to have Zac pulsing cum into Chris's hand, before feeding it to him. He came to a dead stop, and Zac let out a growl such as Chris had never heard from his lips. Chris smacked his ass, the slap loud and sharp. "We're not done. I just wanna try something new."

"As long as it involves your tongue and my ass," Zac flung back at him.

Chris laughed. "Never fear, Ass Boy. Yeah, that's gonna be my new name for you. Ass Boy." He lay diagonally across the bed, his head at the corner. "Now sit astride my chest, facing the headboard. Like you're sitting on my face."

Chris had never seen Zac move so fast.

"Like this?" Zac's ass was right where Chris wanted it, his knees to the mattress, his feet bracketing Chris's head.

"Perfect." He pulled Zac's cheeks apart and slowly licked over his hole.

Zac was having none of it. He began to rock back and forth, his breathing shallow and erratic, and Chris speared him with his tongue, pushing a little deeper each time, until Zac was writhing on his tongue. Zac shifted position until he was virtually sitting on Chris's chest, Chris's shoulders pinned beneath him, with Zac in constant motion.

My tongue is gonna hurt like a son of a bitch tomorrow. Not to mention my jaw.

Zac's movements sped up, and tremors rippled through him. "Chris…"

"Come on me," Chris demanded. "Come on, shoot all over me. Lemme feel it."

Zac arched, and Chris caught his breath at the sight of Zac's narrow waist, the curve of his spine as warmth spattered Chris's torso, the sound of Zac's soft cries that rebounded around the bedroom.

Then Zac moved, all sinews and toned flesh, and Chris had his arms full once again. "There's something not right here," Zac said breathlessly. "I've come twice tonight, and you haven't come once." And before Chris could suggest that Zac do something about that situation, Zac's mouth was on his cock, swallowing him to the root.

"Holy fuck." Chris shot like a geyser, and Zac took every drop, until Chris was squirming with each suck of his overly sensitive dick. "Jesus."

Zac pulled free of his cock and moved to lean over him, grinning. "I thought it was Ass Boy. But that's okay. Jesus works too." And then their lips met in a slow, sweet kiss, while Chris did his best to hold onto the pleasurable sensations coursing through his body. Zac lay on top of him, and Chris stroked his hands up and down Zac's back.

Finally Zac raised his head and smiled. "I may not want your dick in my ass, but I'll take your tongue any day." He sighed happily. "So where next?"

"Are we talking geographically or metaphorically?" Chris inquired, blissed out from his orgasm. "Because right now I'm not even contemplating moving. Except to get into this bed. With you."

Zac beamed. "That sounds great. But I guess I meant metaphorically. What's next for us? Is this it? We've been there, done all that, bought the T-shirt and gotten ourselves into a relationship?"

Chris chuckled. "Trust me, we're not done. Remember the night we met?"

"How could I forget?"

"I told you then you're not totally vanilla. That you like your sex with a bit of kink."

"And we've seen lots of it," Zac commented.

Chris gave a slow nod. "Seen. Yes. Participated in, no. Maybe it's time to take a step out of your comfort zone. We both know what your parameters are, and we won't move beyond those. But there must be things you'd like to try."

Zac caught his breath. "Simon mentioned a BDSM club. Could… could we go there?"

Chris really like that idea. "Oh, I think we can arrange that."

Playing with Zac was one thing. Adding others into the equation created a completely different dynamic, and Chris couldn't wait to see how it developed.

WATCH AND LEARN

"My head is about to explode."

"I gotta say, the name of this place worries me a little," Zac joked as they stepped onto the main floor of the club. "The Rack? And how come you've waited until now to bring me here?"

"Because *now* you're ready for it." Chris told him. "That stuff you saw in the summer at Matt's place? You'll see all that here, and more. What I'm *hoping* is, you see something you want to try."

"Seeing might be a little difficult," Zac teased. The lighting was dim and the walls and floor were black. Here and there were spotlights, and the smell of sweat and sex filled the air. All around them were men of varying shapes and sizes, not that Zac could see any physical specifics, due to the insufficient light. Some wore leather, others jeans and a harness, and a *lot* of them were naked, but everyone wore boots. One glance at the floor was enough to work out why.

"How come I never knew this place existed?" Zac asked. "I mean, I've walked through the old Meatpacking District a hundred times, and I never even suspected what this was."

"Make the most of it."

"What do you mean?" Zac leaned closer to hear Chris above the music that pumped out of speakers all around them.

"Clubs like this are on the way out. You wait. Ten years from now when this whole neighborhood has been gentrified, the storefront entry to this place will contain one of those boutiques. You know the ones I mean, with ten dresses carefully spaced out on racks, and a bored sales lady working on commission ignoring customers. Only then the place will be called 'Off the Rack.'"

Zac thought that sounded awful. "Then let's enjoy it while it's here." He glanced down at his leather shorts. "Do I look okay?" Chris had bought them for him as a gift, and they were a tight fit. His dick was only half-hard and already it pushed against the zipper.

God help me if I get a hard-on.

"You look edible," Chris said, his voice a little husky.

Zac beamed. "If this means you're gonna eat my ass later, I'm all for that."

Chris snorted. "Yeah, I thought you might be." It was fast becoming Zac's favorite activity when Chris stayed over. And that was something else he could really get used to.

"Chris!" a familiar voice called out. They turned, and Zac recognized Simon from the anniversary party the previous month. He wore a snug-fitting harness across his chest, and boots. Then Zac noticed the metal cock ring, tight around his shaft and balls.

Chris laughed. "Ready for action, I see." He gestured to Zac. "You've met my partner, Zac."

"Sure, at Matt's—*partner?*" Simon's face lit up. "Oh my God." He gave Zac a warm smile. "You must be one exceptional guy."

Zac didn't have a clue how to respond to that.

Simon put his hand to his heart. "Does this mean you're off the market? Damn."

Chris snorted. "There you go, thinking with your little head as usual. No, it does *not*. We're not exclusive, but we only play with others when we're together." When Simon rubbed his hands together gleefully, Chris laughed. "Down boy. Tonight is all about Zac. It's his first visit here." He put his arm around Zac's shoulders.

"And are you here to look—or play?" Simon inquired.

Before Chris could speak for him, Zac blurted out, "Play." Chris leaned in and kissed his neck, and Zac shivered.

"Want to take a look around the place first?" Simon grinned. "It may give you a few ideas what you want to try first."

Zac nodded eagerly. In particular, he wanted to get a closer look at the far end of the floor, where there seemed to be a sort of platform or stage. "What's going on over there?"

Chris chuckled. "Let's go investigate." He and Simon flanked Zac as they made their way across the floor, past men engaged in various acts of flogging, whipping, and a whole lotta fucking. When they got to the stage, Zac had to squeeze through to get a peek.

On the platform were three men, and two of them were naked. One was standing, getting a blowjob from another who was bent over. The third guy, who wore a harness, was spreading gloopy-looking stuff through Bent Guy's crack. Then he slid two gloved fingers into Bent Guy's ass.

The latex glove told Zac instantly what was about to happen.

Simon leaned in. "Is that something you might like?"

Zac shook his head so violently, he was surprised it didn't come off. He watched as Glove Guy penetrated Bent Guy's with four fingers, and all the while Bent

Guy sucked off Standing Guy, moaning around his dick as Harness Guy stretched him out.

"Okay, I've seen enough. Show me something else."

Simon laughed. "Okay, enough fisting. Do you already have an idea in mind?"

"I do," Chris piped up. Zac jerked his head to stare at him, and Chris grinned. "Yes, I know it's your choice, but there's something I think you might *really* like."

"And what's that?"

Chris tugged him away from the stage, Simon coming with them. Chris pulled him in close, moving in to speak into his ear. "Ever had a prostate massage?" Zac caught his breath, and Chris chuckled. "Gonna take that as a no. And before you ask, it'll be *way* better than your experiences with anal. If someone is just straight fucking you, the chance of their dick hitting the prostate is rare—unless they're *really* aiming for it, to make it as pleasurable for you as possible." He looked Zac in the eye. "Has that been your experience?"

Zac snorted. "Fuck no." And now he wanted to know how it felt. He'd fingered himself, of course, but maybe it would feel different if someone else was doing it.

"And in the spirit of trying new things..." Chris grabbed Simon by the arm and tugged him closer. "Si, do you think you could manage to give Zac here a prostate massage while I hold him?"

Simon gave a wide smile. "Ooh, yeah."

Chris lifted Zac's chin with his fingers. "If that's okay with you, of course."

Zac took a deep breath, trying his best to get his racing heart to calm the fuck down, while the steady feed of thumping music throbbed through the floor, just loud enough to be able to hear the grunts and moans that filled the air, accompanied by the odd *thwack* of leather meeting flesh, and the slap of skin against skin.

"You don't have to do this," Chris said quietly.

Zac swallowed. "But I want to." The thought of Chris holding him and talking to him throughout the process went a long way to firming his resolve. "Let's do it."

"Over there." Simon pointed to an unoccupied sling near the wall. "Chris, you stand behind it, and Zac, in you get."

They followed him to the sling, and Chris held it steady while Zac climbed into it and lay on his back. Simon glanced down at Zac's crotch. "Shorts off."

Zac's fingers trembled a little as he lowered the zipper, his cock springing free. He squirmed out of the tight garment, and Chris eased the shorts over his boots, removing them completely. He helped Zac insert his legs into the stirrups which hooked under his knees, his legs in the air. Zac grabbed the chains and held on, his heartbeat racing.

Chris leaned over, and his lips brushed against Zac's ear. "Do you remember what to say if you want to stop?" he murmured.

Zac nodded. "Red."

"Good boy." The warm note in Chris's voice sent a wave of calm through him.

"Zac?" Simon stroked Zac's thigh. "Shift your ass forward a little." Zac did as he was instructed. "There. Perfect."

"Hey." Zac turned his head, and Chris kissed him, a long, sensual kiss that said, 'I'm right here,' 'You've got this', and 'I'm not going to let you go.' Then Chris broke the kiss, and Zac faced Simon.

"Ready." He took a couple of deep breaths, willing himself to be calm.

Simon stroked a single finger down Zac's erect dick. "You have a beautiful cock." He cupped Zac's balls, then held his shaft firmly around its base. He reached for a bottle of clear liquid, which he opened one-handed and held over the head of Zac's dick, letting the cool substance trickle down the shaft. It was less viscous than lube, with the consistency of an oil, and it felt great.

Simon played with the head of Zac's cock, so lightly that it made him shiver. Then he held Zac's balls while he leisurely stroked up and down Zac's shaft.

"Does that feel good?" Chris whispered.

"God, yes." Then Zac groaned as Simon wrapped both hands around his dick, twisting them in opposite directions. "Oh fuck…"

"Play with his nipples," Simon instructed Chris. Zac moaned as Chris flicked his nipples with his thumbs, and the sensation zapped through him right to his cock.

"Fuck, what are you doing to me?" Zac groaned.

"Turning you on," Simon replied. He slid his hands up and down Zac's shaft in different directions, meeting in the middle. "The more aroused you are, the more the prostate swells, making it easier to feel. And it's gonna feel *so* good." Then he resumed playing with Zac's balls, while he picked up speed with the other hand, working the shaft.

Chris tweaked Zac's nipples, and there it was again, that electricity zinging through him, directly linking them to his dick. "Ready for a finger?" Chris asked him.

Zac gaped at him. "Yes!"

Simon laughed. "Well, that was pretty emphatic." He squeezed more of the oil onto his fingers, then stroked them over Zac's hole, sending ripples of pleasure through his body. "Here we go."

Zac held his breath as Simon slowly penetrated him, his thumb under Zac's balls, his middle finger sliding into him easy as anything. Simon kept it still while he stroked Zac's cock, until Zac was squirming in the sling, wanting him to get a fucking move on.

"You're so warm inside," Simon told him. "So tight around my finger." Then he moved it ever so slightly, and Zac gasped, a jolt going through him.

"Oh my fucking God, do that again."

Simon did, and Zac rocked his hips a little, wanting more. Simon made tiny movements with his finger, while he rubbed over the head of his cock with a slick palm.

It was like exquisite torture. Violent shudders wracked Zac's body, and Chris held him. "It's okay, baby. You look so fucking beautiful, the way you move when he strokes you inside."

Zac forced himself to breathe regularly, conscious of wave upon wave of pleasure washing over him, each one bringing him closer and closer to the edge. But every time he thought he was about to come, Simon backed off, withdrawing his fingers and stroking his dick, until Zac was ready to go again.

He was lost in a delicious cycle of bliss as Simon settled in to a pattern: long strokes up and down his cock, alternating with one single long finger inside him, rubbing over his gland until he thought his head was about to explode; and then another retreat to let Zac catch his breath. And through it all, Chris held him, told him how amazing he looked, how well he was doing, how fucking awesome his orgasm was going to be—assuming Simon was going to let him come.

Finally, Simon stroked a gentle slick hand over Zac's cock and balls. "Not gonna stop this time. Okay?"

Zac nodded, his heart pounding. Chris leaned over and kissed him, murmuring against his lips, "Can't wait to see you shoot your load."

Simon slid his middle finger into Zac's hole, and Zac moaned as he stroked and rubbed Zac's gland, his other hand working Zac's shaft, only not as leisurely as before: they were heading for the finish line.

Zac was shaking, the sling moving with him as he danced on Simon's finger, his dick like a rock, his balls tight. "Chris," he called out, unable to keep still.

"I've got you." Chris covered Zac's hand with his, his gaze locked on Zac's face. And when it came, violent shudders jolted Zac as he shot over his chest, so forceful that it hit his chin and cheek. Chris bent over to lick up his cum, and shared it with Zac in a lingering kiss as Zac rode the wave of his climax.

"How was it?" Chris asked, stroking Zac's hair away from his head.

Zac shivered. "Never felt anything so intense. It was as if I felt it through my whole body."

Simon wiped his hands on a paper towel, then came to stand next to Zac's head. "Thank you."

Zac gaped at him. "Why are you thanking *me*? Surely it should be the other way around."

Simon bent over and kissed him on the lips, a sweet, chaste kiss. "Thank you for letting me be a part of this. You're beautiful when you come." His eyes sparkled. "And one day I'd love to play with both of you, if that's okay."

Zac took in Simon's brown eyes, neat beard, and broad chest. "It's okay by me," he said with a smile. He reached down to run his fingers along Simon's heavy cock, pausing at his slit from which precum spooled down in a glistening silken thread. Zac rubbed his thumb over the head and brought the clear liquid to his own lips. He licked it slowly, noting Simon's dilated pupils and the hitch in his breathing.

Simon grinned and glanced at Chris. "Your man learns fast." He leaned over to kiss Zac once more, sharing the taste.

When he straightened, Zac wrapped his fingers around Simon's dick. "I'd love to see Chris taking this up his ass." He snuck a peek at Chris. "Although I think Chris already knows what it feels like."

Chris's lips met his in a kiss that sent warmth spreading through him in a languid wave. "And the next time I feel it? I want your mouth around my dick while he fucks me."

"As long as you're eating my ass at the same time, fine." Zac could picture it in his head, clear as anything.

Chris laughed. "Oh my God. I've created a monster."

Simon grinned. "A very flexible monster. And I for one wanna try that out."

Zac let out a happy sigh.

"What just went through your mind?" Chris asked, his hand gentle on Zac's cheek.

"Just thinking about how much I've learned since I met you."

Chris kissed his forehead. "Baby, we've only just begun."

Zac had no idea of the time. A little light penetrated Chris's blinds, enough to see by, and there was the constant hum of traffic from outside. He was warm, enveloped in Chris's arms.

He was happier than he'd ever been.

"Why're you awake?" Chris said sleepily.

"Something woke me up. Go back to sleep."

Chris stroked his arm. "God, you smell good."

Zac chuckled. "That's *your* bodywash you're smelling."

"Wow. Do I always smell like this?" Chris nuzzled his neck, and that was all it took for Zac's cock to take an interest. Judging by the hot hard dick nestled in Zac's crease, Chris's was doing the same. Chris rocked, a gentle motion of his hips that slid his shaft up and down.

Okay, now Zac was *really* awake.

He rolled onto his back. "Get on top of me," he whispered.

Chris chuckled. "I thought last night had wiped you out. Obviously I was wrong." He covered Zac with his body, undulating a little. "Oh, *someone's* hard." Then his lips were on Zac's, and Zac opened for him, loving the feel of Chris's weight on him.

"Three firsts in one night," he murmured when Chris broke the kiss. Chris's mouth was on his neck, kissing and sucking, and Zac shivered.

Chris paused. "Three?"

"Uh-huh. My prostate massage, sleeping in your bed instead of the guest room—and this."

"And what *is* this?"

Zac took a step into the unknown. "Well, I'm kinda hoping my boyfriend is going to make love to me."

There was no missing Chris's intake of breath.

Before Zac could speak, Chris's mouth claimed his, and Zac's toes curled at the heat promised in that kiss. Then Chris shifted lower, licking over Zac's nipple with a leisurely tongue.

"Oh, you know I love it when you do that," Zac said with a shiver.

Another wry chuckle. "Which is why I do it." Chris kissed down his torso, pausing as he reached Zac's dick that lay against his belly, fully hard. Chris rubbed his face over the shaft, nuzzling his balls. He buried his nose in the crease between body and thigh, then rubbed his face over Zac's shaft again, before licking a line from root to head.

Zac waited for Chris to take his dick into his mouth, but when Chris didn't, he groaned.

"Patience," Chris murmured as he crawled up Zac's body again, rubbing his stubbled jaw over Zac's abs and pecs.

"But I want to *come*," Zac remonstrated, hating the touch of a whine in his voice.

"And you're going to," Chris assured him. He rubbed his face against Zac's neck, and began to move, a sensual undulation as he rocked his hips, sliding his heavy cock over Zac's.

Oh fuck.

"How did you know?" Zac demanded.

Chris flicked his nipple with his tongue before answering. "I called Matt to thank him for the talk we had at his place. Then Jake got on the phone and said if I wanted to make you *really* happy…"

Zac sighed. "You have some great friends." Then Chris propped himself up on his hands and started rolling his hips, and Zac let out a low moan. "Fuck, that feels amazing."

"Another first," Chris whispered before kissing him again, only now Zac fed him moans and sighs of pleasure as Chris's shaft rubbed against his. Chris left one hand on the bed and with the other, he took Zac's dick, stroking it in time to match each languid slide of his cock through the crease above Zac's thigh. Chris straddled Zac's leg, his feet rubbing against Zac's as he rocked, unhurried and sexy as hell.

"Aw, fuck." Zac spread his legs and Chris inserted his body between them, still rolling his hips. Zac's hands were on his back, his waist, and finally his ass, grabbing Chris's cheeks and squeezing them. Then he shifted higher, raking his nails down Chris's back, and Chris arched, moaning, the erotic motion of his hips not pausing for a second.

Then everything shifted into a high gear.

Chris sucked on the base of Zac's neck, and Zac knew there'd be a bruise the following day. He rocked faster, faster, and Zac dug his nails into the muscles on Chris's back as Chris propelled him closer and closer to the edge.

"Fuck, oh fuck, yeah, fuck, don't stop," Zac begged as Chris's cock rubbed over his balls and shaft, Zac's whole body tingling as he sought the orgasm he knew was coming. Chris picked up speed, his breathing harsh and shallow as he rolled his hips, and Zac knew he was close too. And when Zac finally came, warmth pooling on his belly below the head of his dick, he cried out, lost in an ocean of sensation, shaking helplessly as he pulsed out the last drops of cum.

"My turn," Chris murmured, before grabbing Zac's thighs and pushing his knees toward his chest. His thick shaft slid over Zac's hole and Chris rocked again, his cock slick with Zac's cum. Chris's breathing quickened, and Zac reached for his face.

"Come. Let me feel you come on my hole," he gasped out as Chris picked up the pace again, setting every nerve alight as he rubbed his solid shaft over Zac's pucker. And when Chris came, trembling in Zac's arms, Zac held him, aware of the warmth fluid that trickled over his skin.

Zac clung to him, both of them breathing erratically, both shaking. "Oh my God."

Chris chuckled, and kissed his cheek. "Well, if Jesus works for you, I can live with God."

Zac returned his kiss. "And they're both better than Ass Boy." He sighed. "I know we need to clean up, but I don't want to move." The sheet beneath them would have to be changed, for one thing.

Chris kissed his neck. "I feel it too. I don't want this moment to end."

Zac locked his arms around Chris's neck. "But you know what? There will be other moments. This was just the first."

"The first of many," Chris added.

Zac loved the sound of that.

"For me? You shouldn't have." - Take Two.

Eight months later

Chris got out of the shower and sniffed. "That smells amazing," he called to Zac in the kitchen.

"Glad you think so. I had to do something special for your birthday, right?" Zac hollered back.

Chris rubbed the towel briskly over his head, smiling to himself. *I didn't see* this *coming a year ago.* If anyone had told him he'd not only be in a relationship with someone, but also living with him, and gloriously happy about it, he'd have laughed his ass off. Zac moving in with him had been a no-brainer. They were both fed up with the to-ing and fro-ing, and Zac's apartment was too small for them, so this made perfect sense.

There had been several precious milestones in their journey to the present day. Meeting the in-laws—well, the nearest thing Chris would ever have to them—had been nerve-wracking beforehand, but he had to admit, Zac had their reaction nailed. They took to Chris instantly, and he to them. They didn't care about the age difference, not that Zac seemed to have ever cared about it either.

The sweetest day had to have been Christmas. They were still living apart then, but Zac spent his days off at Chris's place. Waking up Christmas morning, with his arms full of a sleeping Zac had been wonderful enough.

Having Zac roll over, rub his eyes, smile, and say 'I love you' had been the best present ever.

Chris pulled on his jeans, grabbed a clean shirt, and went to investigate what culinary delights Zac had in store for him.

The kitchen smelled of fried chicken, and Chris inhaled deeply. "My favorite."

Zac jerked his head up from chopping salad and blinked. He shifted quickly to stand in front of the table. "Well, it *is* your birthday."

"And I'm sure your fried chicken will be just as delicious as that place on Eight Avenue we love so much." Zac's sudden movement was extremely suspicious. Chris glanced around the kitchen then peered under the kitchen table behind Zac's legs. He snorted. "I see it will."

Zac widened his eyes. "I was running late. And I happened to be passing by, so I thought why not?"

Chris gave him a hard stare. "Your trip home takes you nowhere near it. Come on, confession time. You were gonna hide the bags and pretend you'd made it, weren't you?"

"How was I to know you'd take the fastest shower in history?"

Chris walked up to him and cupped Zac's face in his hands. "Have I told you recently how much I love you?"

Zac pretended to think. "Hmm. Maybe you'd better tell me again, to be on the safe side."

Chris leaned in and kissed him, Zac's lips parting to let him in. Chris slid his hands down Zac's back, cupping and squeezing his ass. When they parted, he murmured. "Love you."

Zac's eyes shone. "Love you too. And one of these days, you'll have to teach me to cook like you."

Chris laughed. "We all have our strengths. One of mine happens to be cooking."

"And what's my strength?" Zac demanded.

Chris grinned. "Cock sucking. And after dinner, you can demonstrate how proficient you really are."

Zac bit his lip in that way Chris always found sexy as fuck. "Who says we have to wait until then?"

As he lowered himself to his knees, Chris sighed happily. "Happy birthday to me."

When Zac came back into the living room, the dishwasher loaded and running, Chris finally ran out of patience. "Where's my present?"

Zac laughed. "Hang on, Oh Impatient One." He grabbed a brightly colored bag from behind the couch and handed it over.

Chris narrowed his gaze. "This isn't gonna be like last year, is it?"

Zac chuckled. "No Viagra this time. That's the last thing you need."

Chris opened the bag and removed the oblong case. When he opened it, he gasped. "Aw. A set of sounds." Eight metal sounds of varying degrees of thickness, some of them slightly curved, nestled in the red velvet-lined zipped case.

"Well, you did say you wanted to try it."

Chris kissed him exuberantly on the cheek. "They're perfect." Then he realized the bag wasn't empty. He peered into it. "Aw. A tube of surgilube too. You thought of everything." He grinned. "Well, at least I know what we're doing tonight."

The doorbell rang, and Zac raised one finger. "Hold that thought." He went to answer it.

"If it's someone selling something, tell them we're not interested," Chris whispered loudly. He gazed at the shiny metal sounds, a shiver rippling through him at the sight of the thickest one. *I'm sure gonna feel that.*

The door opened, and in walked Matt, Jake, and Simon, Zac behind them. Chris gaped. "Hey, guys." He peered at Zac. "Did you organize a surprise party for me?"

Zac snickered. "Not exactly a party." He gestured to Simon, who stepped forward and took the sounds case from Chris's hands.

"Hey, that's *my* present," he complained.

"I know," Simon replied. "And *I'm* the one who's gets to play with them first. Only, it'll be *your* dick they're going in." He glanced at Matt and Jake. "Well, what are you waiting for? Strip the birthday boy."

Chris stared at Zac. "For me? Aww, you shouldn't have." He lurched up off the couch and pulled Zac into his arms. "God, I love you," he whispered.

"Love you too," Zac whispered back. "And trust me, I'm going to enjoy your present as much as you do. I get to watch you take one." His eyes twinkled. "In fact, I'll be taking notes. Because the next time? It'll be me doing it."

Chris laughed. "In that case? Watch and learn."

About the author

K.C. Wells lives on an island off the south coast of the UK, surrounded by natural beauty. She writes about men who love men, and can't even contemplate a life that doesn't include writing.

The rainbow rose tattoo on her back with the words 'Love is Love' and 'Love Wins' is her way of hoisting a flag. She plans to be writing about men in love - be it sweet and slow, hot or kinky - for a long while to come.

Other titles

Learning to Love
Michael & Sean
Evan & Daniel
Josh & Chris
Final Exam

Sensual Bonds
A Bond of Three
A Bond of Truth

Merrychurch Mysteries
Truth Will Out
Roots of Evil
A Novel Murder

Love, Unexpected
Debt
Burden

Dreamspun Desires
The Senator's Secret
Out of the Shadows
My Fair Brady
Under The Covers

Lions & Tigers & Bears
A Growl, a Roar, and a Purr

Love Lessons Learned
First

Waiting for You
Step by Step
Bromantically Yours
BFF

Collars & Cuffs
An Unlocked Heart
Trusting Thomas
Someone to Keep Me (K.C. Wells & Parker Williams)
A Dance with Domination
Damian's Discipline (K.C. Wells & Parker Williams)
Make Me Soar
Dom of Ages (K.C. Wells & Parker Williams)
Endings and Beginnings (K.C. Wells & Parker Williams)

Secrets – with Parker Williams
Before You Break
An Unlocked Mind
Threepeat
On the Same Page

Personal
Making it Personal
Personal Changes
More than Personal
Personal Secrets
Strictly Personal
Personal Challenges

Personal – The Complete Series

Confetti, Cake & Confessions

Connections
Saving Jason
A Christmas Promise
The Law of Miracles
My Christmas Spirit
A Guy for Christmas

Island Tales
Waiting for a Prince
September's Tide
Submitting to the Darkness

Lightning Tales
Teach Me
Trust Me
See Me
Love Me

A Material World
Lace
Satin
Silk
Denim

Southern Boys
Truth & Betrayal
Pride & Protection
Desire & Denial

Maine Men
Finn's Fantasy
Ben's Boss

Kel's Keeper
Here For You
Sexting The Boss
Gay on a Train
Sunshine & Shadows
Watch and Learn
My Best Friend's Brother
Bears in the Woods
Double or Nothing
Back from the Edge
Lose to Win
Teasing Tim
Switching it up
Out for You
State of Mind

Anthologies

Fifty Gays of Shade
Winning Will's Heart

Come, Play
Watch and Learn

Writing as Tantalus
Damon & Pete: Playing with Fire